Marilyn E. Burrows became enthused with writing at an early age. She had many mentors along the way with the most notable ones being a few teachers in her final years of high school. Along the way, she has worked in business (as a proprietor) as well as working in the social services field as a front-line worker. Working with such a diverse set of people only increased her desire to create worlds in which they grow and prosper.

Her parents were prairie folk who moved to the West Coast before she was born. Within her first few years of life, they had to deal with things they never dreamed of, such as a major tsunami and a culture that differed from the one they had grown up in.

She still resides on the West Coast with her husband, Doug and their two kittens. Her adult children live nearby.

Marilyn E. Burrows

When the River Calls

Austin Macauley Publishers®
London * Cambridge * New York * Sharjah

Ordering Information
Quantity sales: Special discounts are available on quantity purchases by corporations, associations, and others. For details, contact the publisher at the address below.

Publisher's Cataloging-in-Publication data
Burrows, Marilyn E.
When the River Calls

ISBN 9798895432044 (Paperback)
ISBN 9798895432051 (ePub e-book)

Library of Congress Control Number: 2025906963

www.austinmacauley.com/us

First Published 2025
Austin Macauley Publishers LLC
40 Wall Street, 33rd Floor, Suite 3302
New York, NY 10005
USA

mail-usa@austinmacauley.com
+1 (646) 5125767

I thank those at Austin Macauley who have worked closely with me over the past several years. It's not always easy but it makes a difference.

Chapter One

It was getting near sunset as Emma got home from her walk around the river. The warm air brushed against her face as she walked up to the door of the cottage. She was glad to be home so she could take the braces off her legs. Giving each of her grandparents a hug, she continued to her bedroom. Then, it was into the shower. There was pain forming in her legs. She loved being able to walk down the river again; each surgery had brought her closer to living pain-free. It seemed forever since she had lost the normal use of her legs. Sometimes, she even had trouble remembering life before. Her doctors felt the memory loss was due to the car incident. She had to admit that not remembering could be helpful at times.

Emma let the warm water wash over her. She loved the fact that her grandparents had moved, from the mainland to Allerton, to allow her to finish school. It had meant them giving up their lives on the mainland, but she never heard them complain. This year she would graduate. She still hadn't completely made up her mind about a design school or how far away she would be willing to go.

Back in her bedroom, she wondered how they could call this place a cottage. It was big, three storeys high. Her grandparents had decorated it elegantly. They had even made her a studio on the top floor where she went to draw, or sketch, or design clothes. But she had another corner up there, where her mother's unfinished painting hung. Beside the closet was the canvas, where she had started some sketches. If all went well, she wanted to finish her painting and give it to Junior when he graduated from his engineering programme. He was scheduled to finish his programme this year as well.

Emma looked at her prom dress, wondering what her mom would have thought. It was pale lavender with a gentle fit that covered her braces. Justin had asked her to be his date to the prom. Her family still wanted her to keep her distance from him, even though it had been several years since the whole mess with her father and Justin's mother.

She finished drying off, put on some comfortable clothes, then headed back downstairs. When she reached the landing, she saw a box sitting there. It had no name on it, so she continued downstairs. Her grandmother met her at the bottom of the stairs and asked her if she saw the box on the landing.

"I did, Grandma, but there was no name on the box."

"It was addressed to you. Why don't you bring it down and open it?" her grandma encouraged.

"OK," Emma said as she went back to the landing to grab the parcel.

Her grandpa was in the living room, so she headed that way. When she got there, her grandpa looked up from his newspaper and smiled. He never got over the way Emma's eyes looked just like her mother's. Emma propped the box up on the coffee table as she carefully unwrapped it. It was a weird shape. By the time she got all the paper off, it looked like a curled-up towel. It wasn't a towel though. It was a painter's canvas, so she kept unrolling it to see what was on the canvas. With each unfolding, she held her breath a little more until the painting was completely unrolled. She sat there staring at the canvas in silence. Her grandma came over to look down at the canvas.

"Goodness, Emma, this is the painting of your dad. Your mother painted it. It sold at the art show that your dad put on just after she passed."

Emma kept looking down at the painting, staring into her dad's eyes. It was both beautiful and haunting. She turned the box over to see where it came from, but all that was visible was a set of numbers. The address was from out of the country.

They never did find out who purchased the picture. Emma had started her own sketching when she returned from the hospital on the mainland. It gave her an opportunity to gain better hand-control as well as a way to sketch out the things that kept clouding in on her. Emma still had a numb spot inside from when her dad had been killed. He didn't hunt himself, but he had been out with Casey and Raymond. He wanted to help them, so he had packed their meals and carried the extra equipment. Things didn't end well.

"Grandpa, can we get this framed somewhere? Is there somewhere in town that would do that?"

"I'm not sure, Emma. I'll look around tomorrow. If not here, I know someone on the mainland that could frame it."

"Thanks, Grandpa," Emma replied.

Her grandma came in with a tray of goodies. It was nearing bedtime, so they sat and talked about their day. Emma told them about the seals down at the marina. They still amazed her with their water skills. She also told them about the seagulls that kept diving at the seals to steal the fish, and how the seals did their little underwater duck. The seagulls ended up going away empty-handed.

Emma hoped she never had to leave her hometown, but she knew that if she wanted to go to design school, it could mean going to the mainland. Her art teacher had given her a couple of online schools to check out. She decided to do that this weekend.

"Have you decided if you'll go to the prom with Tim yet?"

"I'm not sure, Grandma, it would be like taking my dad to the prom. But from where I sit, that isn't all bad."

"Raymond Gray also asked if you would like to go with him. He is only a couple years older than Junior."

"I know. I'm still thinking about it. I know I need to make a decision soon."

"Don't let it upset you, Emma. Either of the two would be a good escort for you."

"I know, Grandpa. I'm just not sure."

Emma finished her snack then headed upstairs to get into pyjamas. She thought about going to work on her designs or to do a little painting, but she was feeling quite tired. While she was lying down on her bed, Ziggy cuddled up beside her. Junior had asked her to take care of Ziggy, as he lived in a no-pets flat closer to his university. Her dad's parents still lived in the Ryan house. Emma was glad that they wanted to stay close. Junior ended up there a lot. Her dog, Scout, lived there with them.

Emma sat up, picked up her journal and began to write. Her counsellor had told her that writing things out could help you understand your day. That had been nearly seven years ago, but she still enjoyed writing it all down. Her big conundrum right now was, who to choose to take her to the prom. If it were totally her decision she would go with Justin. However, the past seemed to be framing the present.

Justin hadn't been part of the events that happened with her dad in the hospital. In fact, he had been staying with the Gray family at that time. All Justin had now was his mother, who had spent a few years in the Mental Health Recovery Centre. Justin had stayed with the Gray family for a while and had lived for a brief time with his mother after she was released from the centre. Things didn't work out well, so Justin went back to living at the Gray house while his mother went back to the centre. He and Emma often walked the river together. They enjoyed spending time together.

Emma finished with her journal then turned the light off. She cuddled Ziggy, falling asleep with him still in her arms.

Justin watched the sunset while sitting at the beach near Emma's house. It wasn't the right time to pursue her with all the bad blood between the two families, but heaven help anyone who tried to mess with her. Getting on his bike, he headed back to the Gray house. He was thankful that Elin still took in young people. It was the best place he had ever lived. She had called about half an hour ago to ask if he would be home for dinner. He told her he would be about an hour, so she had offered to hold onto dinner for him. Her kindness always seemed a little surreal, as it was nothing like the life he had growing up.

Justin still missed his brother Trevor, but found it hard to think the same way about their father. His mother worked with Elliot Hayes after his dad passed away. That is how the bad blood between the families started. Elliot had convinced his mom that Emma's dad had caused the death of his brother and his dad. He had encouraged her to find Emma's dad and make him pay.

His mother was now in a first stage house at the centre. From what he had been told, she was doing quite well.

Justin pulled into Elin's driveway and locked up his bike. Junior had left him the bike when he went off to university. It's kind of weird how he had become friends with Junior, or Jason, as he now liked to be called. Jason had even stood by him when Justin's dad had tried to take out Tim Bryan down at the Y, as well as after his brother, Trevor, had harassed the Ryan family so intensely. That is why he felt so protective of Emma. It was his brother, Trevor, who forced her family's car off the road. It caused the death of her mother as well as injuries to the other three in the car. No one would get a chance to hurt her again, not with him around.

Elin looked out the window and saw Justin was home, so she put his dinner in the microwave. Many young people had stayed at the Gray house, but Justin was a little more difficult to read than most. He came in and headed to the washroom to wash up. The smell of his dinner drifted along to the washroom, so he quickly headed back to the kitchen.

"Dinner is on the table, Justin. Good thing you got back when you did, it's getting quite dark."

"Thanks for dinner, Elin. Emma and I went for a walk along the river, then we chatted for a while. Afterwards I decided to watch the sunset, down by the river."

"Sounds good. How's Emma doing?"

"OK. She's a little stressed about prom. I told Jason I would keep it a secret that he was coming home to take her."

"Good plan. He will be home in a couple of days, then?"

"Yes, his Ryan-side grandparents have the house all prepared. They are planning a big 'surprise' party for Emma."

"Are you going?"

"I'm not sure yet. I don't want to mess it up for her."

"Talk to Jason, let him make the decision. I think Emma would like you to be there."

"I hope so."

"She does, but her father taught her well."

"Right, you knew her dad. Do you think he would approve of me?"

"Probably not, but just because, he would have a tough time approving of anyone that dated his daughter. You're a good kid, Justin. Don't forget that."

Justin finished his supper then got up to do his dishes. Elin watched him, hoping that Jason would understand the confusion that Justin felt about the Ryan family. Jason was one of the few people who could get through to Justin. He had doggedly stood up for him amid the unkindness that followed Justin. His parents had made his life difficult, sometimes without even realising it. His mother, Adrianne, was still on the recovery trail. Hopefully, she would make it all the way this time. Justin finished his dishes, then headed to his bedroom. He was feeling tired but decided to see if he could get in touch with Jason.

Sitting on his bed, Justin sent a text to Jason to see if he was available for a phone chat. He waited a few minutes, then decided to get ready for bed. He pulled on his pyjamas and was heading to the washroom when his phone started to buzz.

"Hi, Jason," Justin answered.

"Hey, Justin. Is everything OK? You usually don't ask for a phone chat."

"Everything is OK. I'm just a little uncertain about attending the party you are putting on for Emma. I don't want to mess up anything."

"I have talked with both sets of grandparents. They know you will be there. They also know how important it is to Emma that you are there. It will be a good place for you to be, I promise."

"OK. Thanks, Jason. I look forward to your being here. Maybe we can slip away for a coffee sometime, if you have any free time."

"That's a plan," Jason replied. "We will set the time and date as soon as I get to Allerton."

"Looking forward to it. Thanks, Jason, for everything."

"You're welcome, my friend. Thanks for caring about Emma."

Justin clicked his phone off. Tomorrow he would do laundry to make sure he had decent clothes for the party. Prom was coming in two days, but the party was the day after prom. Why was he so worked up about all this? He and Emma got along really well. Besides, Jason was, and still is, one of his best friends. He had to get to sleep as he worked at the coffee house tomorrow morning. He turned off his light as he fell into bed.

Emma woke early and headed for the washroom. She looked at herself in the mirror, wondering if her scars would ever go away. There was a face surgery planned for this summer; it would be her final surgery. But first, there was the surgery on her knees. Hopefully, she wouldn't need any more braces.

Anyway, today was Friday, so school would be let out early as they prepared for prom. Jason was supposed to be home today or tomorrow, she looked forward to seeing him. Over the past few years, it had been great to have Jason, or Junior as she still thought of him, close by. He could make her smile just by being there. He reminded her of their days with her mom and dad.

Emma went to her room to dress for school. She chose a pair of slacks and a cool top as the temperature had started to climb lately. Grabbing her braces, she headed downstairs for breakfast. Halfway down, she could smell breakfast and she realised how hungry she felt. She headed for the kitchen. Her grandma looked up as she came into sight.

"Good morning, Grandma."

"Good morning, Emma, you look ready for school."

"Yup. Just breakfast, then putting on the metal."

"Junior called last night. He will be home tonight so both sets of grandparents are planning to have dinner together."

"Sounds amazing! I can't wait to see him."

"Oh, your grandpa is going to drive you to school. Then he'll look around for someone to frame your picture. That takes care of two birds with one trip."

"That would be great. I don't mind taking the bus but it's always fun to go with grandpa."

Her grandpa walked into the kitchen. He saw his two girls talking and decided to take out the dishes for breakfast.

"I heard grandma tell you that I can take you to school today. That is, if you are up to it," he said with a smile.

"Of course. It's always fun to be with you, Grandpa."

"It hasn't always been easy for you, but it's incredibly satisfying to see how well you and Jason are doing. Jeff, could you grab the milk from the fridge, please," her grandma added.

"Sure thing," her grandpa answered.

They all found seats at the table. When Emma was finished, she left to wash up in the downstairs washroom. Then she fitted on her braces. Her trousers were loose enough to fit over them. She smiled, as she had made the trousers herself. As she wandered into the kitchen, she saw her grandparents cleaning off the table. Her grandpa went to the closet to grab a jacket before he and Emma headed out to the car.

On the way to school, grandpa asked lots of questions about school. Emma could tell that he was wondering what the near future would hold. She would have liked to give him answers, if she had any to give. She loved the fact that he was interested in what she was planning. He dropped her off at the school and told her that grandma would text her, if they found a local framer. She smiled, giving him a hug as the first bell rang.

Her first class was an Applied Design class, which was close to her locker. She got her supplies, making it to the classroom door just as the second bell rang. Sitting down at her desk, she looked over to see that her project was still hanging in the finishing room. Time was running out, so she hoped to spend a couple of her lunch hours in here, ploughing through.

Jason finished his classes for the day and jumped into his car to head to Allerton. It had been several weeks since he had been there. He had to admit he was a little homesick today. These were the days when he really missed his mom and dad, Emma too. He couldn't believe that Emma was completing high school this year; plus, she had started thinking about plans to go on to design school in the autumn. He had another few months until he finished his degree. He was already looking for possible employers. It was a good hour's drive so Jason pulled into a petrol station to fill up his vehicle. As he got back into his vehicle, a young guy came up to him asking where he was going. They chatted for a while.

"Where are you headed?" Jason asked the young guy.

"Just an hour down the road, I live with my parent there. I just took a bus here to see some friends."

"So, you're taking the bus home?"

"Yes, and here it comes. Thanks for the chat break, I was starting to feel a little alone."

"No problem. Can I ask your name? My name is Jason Ryan."

"Andrew Sullivan."

"Well Andrew, if you get to Allerton, look me up. I think I'm still in the phone book, but here is my mobile phone number."

"Thanks, Jason. I better get on board."

"Bye, Andrew."

Jason started his car and headed home. He so appreciated how his grandparents had stepped in, when the bottom fell out. First losing his mother, then his dad. There was no darker period in all his days as then. He remembered staying with Elin, as the estate was all worked out. He was so amazed that both grandparents were willing to stay in Allerton until they finished school. He wondered if they would head home now, or not. Whatever happened, he was grateful for their efforts to make life as normal as possible.

But this weekend was all about Emma. She had accomplished so much despite the surgeries and the circumstances. There was a rumour that her high school teachers had nominated her for the Comeback Award. He was so incredibly proud of her.

Jason turned on the music and let the road take him home. He had thought about bringing Rosa with him, but it wouldn't be the easiest place for her to meet his family. She was the softness in his life, full of kindness and grace, which he needed on a continuous basis when the pressures of his classwork boiled over. In ways, she reminded him a bit of his mom who laughed easily, and gave a hug without any reason. Some of his friends had asked Jason if she was 'the one', but he wasn't willing to go there until he was done with classes and had employment.

Jason pulled up to the family home and took a moment to drink in its familiarity. A piece of him was here, it gave him a sense of belonging. He climbed out of his car, using the ramp that he had helped his grandpa build. When he reached the porch, the door flew open, and his grandma gave him a big hug. For some reason, it took all he had, to not start crying. Grandpa was right behind her.

Scout bounded to the door to jump up on him. Scout was a good-size dog, but he still wanted Jason to pick him up. Ever so carefully, he picked up Scout as he sat down on the recliner. Scout was happy with that, so he turned to Jason's face and licked him until Jason put him down. He wondered how Ziggy was doing with Emma, but it was easier for the grandparents having the pets in separate houses.

The house smelled of barbecued food. Jason couldn't help remembering his dad and mom and their far-out barbecues.

His grandparents told him to bring in his luggage, then they could sit for a soda. Jason ripped down the stairs to bring in his suitcase. He also had a gift for his grandparents. He knew they liked to grow things, so he had bought them a greenhouse. If they moved back to their home, they could take it with them. If not, then there was a place out back, they could put it up. He left the greenhouse on the front porch, as it was quite heavy. He would surprise them after he took his luggage upstairs.

Chapter Two

Jason took his suitcase to his room. Looking around he noticed that everything was pretty much as he had left it. After his parents passed, settling the estate had gotten so complicated. He learned that things are more complicated when someone dies without a will, as both his parents had done. It was decided that the house would go into a trust until both he and Emma were of legal age. That worked well, as both sets of his grandparents had decided to stay close until the kids were older. His dad's parents agreed to live in this house. That only happened after they had moved back to their home at one point. That was why Jason spent some time at the Gray house, as he was barely 17 when his dad passed, and he was struggling. During that time, Emma moved in with his mother's parents in their Allerton cottage. Elin had been amazing. He still thought of her as a mentor, as well as a much-wiser sister.

There was a knock on the front door. Jason remembered that he had left the greenhouse on the porch. He ran down to get the door, but his grandpa had gotten there first. It was Emma with his mom's parents. Jason knew there would be talk about what was on the porch, so he started off the conversation.

"Grandpa, I got a small greenhouse for you and grandma. I know how much you enjoy gardening and growing your own food. Whether you stay here or move somewhere else, you will be able to have your own homegrown food."

"Jason, that wasn't necessary. We have loved being part of your life here. I hope it isn't a moving-out present."

"No, not for the a moment. It is just a thank you present. I have something special for grandma and grandpa Ravinser, as well. I will be right back."

Jason ran up the stairs to get the box from his suitcase. Rosa had made the Ravinser grandparents the most beautiful piece of pottery Jason had ever seen. He wasn't too sure how much to say to the grandparents, but he was planning on introducing the subject of Rosa. There was also a small box sitting in his luggage, so he quickly put it in his pocket. He jogged back down the stairs to where the whole family was working at getting dinner on the table. He put the box down where grandpa Ravinser was sitting. His grandpa looked up him and smiled.

"Should I open it now?" he asked.

"Yes, please."

Grandpa Ravinser removed the beautiful paper as he opened the box. He just stared at the item until grandma Ravinser came over to him. She picked up the beautiful vase, turning it around several times.

"It is amazing, Jason. Where did you find something this beautiful?"

"Well, it is a bit of a long story."

"Come on, Junior. Spit it out," Emma said as she laughed a little.

Jason looked over at his sister. Her smile showed that she knew something, he was wondering just how much.

"Well, it was made by a very special friend of mine…"

"It's his girlfriend," Emma said with a giggle. Jason looked at her and frowned.

"Well, Rosa is a close friend of mine. We have been dating for about a year. She is incredibly beautiful as well as talented."

It got noticeably quiet, then Jason looked up from the table to a sea of grins. It had taken so much courage to tell them about her. They all just smiled, asking him more questions than he could even begin to answer. Family was amazing but tiring at the same time. When they were done, they had convinced him to ask her to come to the party on Sunday. But Jason had one more surprise, he reached in his pocket for the little box from his luggage. He gave it to Emma. As she opened the box, she started to cry. Inside was her mother's locket that had been given to her mother by her parents. The grandparents all looked at Emma as she dried her tears.

"Thank you, Junior. It is beautiful."

"Look inside," Jason encouraged her.

She opened the locket. Inside was engraved her name and her mom's name in the shape of a heart.

"It's amazing, Junior. Thank you," Emma said as she hugged Jason.

"There's a few more things. First, I am your official date for the prom. I deserve that honour for putting up with you for so many years."

"That would be amazing."

"And second comes with a condition."

"What would that be?" Emma asked.

"Second, you need to start calling me Jason. Rosa doesn't even know that I have been called Junior."

"OK. For her visit, it will be Jason. What's the other thing?"

"I consulted the family here. We have invited Justin to your party on Sunday."

"Really! Thank you all so much. Justin is one of my best friends."

After the gift opening, everyone parted company. As Jason headed up to his room, he could hear his grandparents cleaning up the dishes, so he decided to go down to help. They smiled when he came into the kitchen. They joked about how he still liked to wash dishes, even though it was now an unpaid task. He smiled, thinking that it would also give him some time to think about the best way to ask Rosa to the party. By the time the dishes were finished, he decided a phone call would be better than a text, so he headed upstairs to make the call.

The phone rang several times. Jason was about to shut down the line when he heard a small voice come across the line.

"Hi, Jason. I'm just in my last class so I can't talk right now. Can I call you back in half an hour?"

"For sure, Rosa, I'll be waiting."

"Thanks, Jason," Rosa answered.

They both shut down their phones. Jason spent some time wondering what the best way to ask her to come to Emma's party would be. He decided to spend some time checking in on his Allerton friends, so he sent out some messages to see if anyone would reply. In only a few minutes, they had all responded and were trying to set up a time to meet. They decided to meet as a group at 2 pm tomorrow in their usual coffee shop. Jason grinned from ear to ear. As he was heading downstairs to get a coffee, his phone rang. It was Rosa.

"Hi, Rosa. How did the class go?"

"Not too bad. I left just after you called, I will need to catch up next week. How's things going with your family?"

"Pretty much as usual. I told them a little about you, they would like to meet you."

"Oh, that sounds promising."

"It is. Emma of course had to tease me about having a girlfriend. The grandparents just grinned."

"Jason, there is something that I should have told you before, but it didn't seem important. Your sister, Emma, friended me on a social media site. I accepted her request. We have been chatting for the last few weeks."

"Rosa! You should have told me. But it's all good. They really want to meet you. Could you come here for Emma's party Sunday?"

"Well…I should tell you that Emma already invited me, but I wasn't sure if you would want me to meet them that way."

"That imp! She gave me such a tough time when I was trying to tell the grandparents about you. Yes, I do want you here. You can take a bus or drive or I could even come to pick you up."

"Hmmm. Those all seem do-able. Except, I am already on my way to Allerton. I decided to accept Emma's invitation, she messaged me just after your supper."

"That is great! Do you want to stay at our family home?"

"Gee, I already promised Emma I would stay with her. I hope that's OK?"

"It's perfect. The grandparents can be a little old-fashioned, this radiates properness."

"Well, I better get back on the road. I should be there by 9:30 pm easily."

"Drive safe. See you soon."

Jason ended the call. He headed downstairs for a coffee and a small chat with the grandparents. He was so excited about Rosa coming. He was hoping that Rosa would go to the prom with them tomorrow night. They would just need one more ticket. He knew that Elin would know how to make that happen, so Jason called Elin.

"Jason! So good to hear from you. I heard that you are in Allerton for the weekend."

"Yes, I am. I'll be taking Emma to the prom, but an unexpected wrinkle came up."

"What's that?"

"A close friend of mine is coming to town tonight. I would like her to go to the prom with Emma and me."

"That would be cool. How about two tickets so Justin can go as well?"

"Elin, I would love that. Can I just run it by the grandparents? It should be fine as Rosa and I will be chaperoning them."

"The tickets will come with the promise that I get to meet Rosa this weekend."

"Of course. You are coming to Emma's party on Sunday?"

"Yes, that would work. Great. Call me back after your talk with the grandparents."

"Will do. Thanks again, Elin."

"You're welcome, my friend."

Jason entered the kitchen just as his grandparents were preparing their evening tea. He remembered that his mom and dad used to do the same thing. A moment of sadness drifted in. He grabbed a cup to join them as he talked about Rosa coming. He mentioned about the prom and Elin's request, that Justin come to the prom with them. They looked up at Jason. They nodded it would be fine as long as they were chaperoned.

There was one more call to make to the other grandparents, but his grandma told him to let her do that. Jason was wise enough to do just that. They finished their tea, then Jason told them he was going for a drive. He wanted to stop by the cottage to see if Rosa was there yet. He hopped in his car and headed down the road. Someone called his phone, but the number didn't look familiar, so he just kept driving. He noticed that they left a message. He would check that after his drive. The river looked beautiful with the sun starting to set on the mountains, this really was the most beautiful place on Earth. Jason decided to park near the river to put everything into perspective. It had been so long since he could just sit and relax.

As the sun slunk behind the mountains, Jason started up his car and headed over to Emma's. He wanted to have a few words with her before Rosa got there. When he drove up to the cottage, there was just his grandparent's car in the driveway. He knocked on the door as his grandpa opened the door.

"Jason, you don't have to knock. This is your home as well as Emma's."

"I know, Grandpa. I just didn't want to show up without warning."

"OK. We just finished talking with your other grandparents. As far as Ruby and I are concerned, Justin can be part of your foursome at the prom."

"Oh, Grandpa. Thank you. How does Emma feel about it?"

"See for yourself."

Jason walked into the living room where he saw Emma cuddled up with Ziggy. She got up to give him the biggest hug ever. Then she sat down and looked at the cat.

"Are you mad at me, Junior?"

"Mad? About what?"

"About Rosa?"

"Not mad, maybe a little bewildered. But glad she is coming to be with us."

Ziggy took that moment to jump off Emma's lap and onto Jason's lap. There was sure to be a few claw marks, but Ziggy quickly settled down, purring himself to sleep. It had been a while since he saw Ziggy, he looked to be doing well. He petted him a little while, then they saw car lights come into the driveway. Jason gently put Ziggy down on the chair. He headed for the front door as Rosa parked her car.

"Jason, I didn't know I would see you tonight. It is sooo good to see you after such a long drive."

"Good to see you too, Rosa. Come, meet my family."

"Grandma, grandpa, this is Rosa. She is my very special friend."

"Get off it, Junior, I mean Jason. She's your girlfriend," Emma said with a giggle.

Rosa started to giggle too. Soon, they were all smiling as they headed into the house. Jason got her suitcase and carried it in for her. Then Emma grabbed it as she showed Rosa to her room, chattering away. In a way, it made Jason feel incredibly good. It felt like the family accepted Rosa.

Emma was growing up too quickly, yet Jason knew that her injuries and all the recovery work had made her strong enough to take on any task. He didn't tell her often enough, how proud he was of her. The two of them came back downstairs. Rosa took Jason's hand as they headed into the living room. It was already getting late, so Jason gave Rosa a quick hug as he told her he would see her in the morning. The grandparents demanded their hugs. By the time he was finished, he had to admit he felt very loved. Emma walked with him to the door, thanking him for being there for her prom night and graduation. All Jason could do was to hold her, as the tears started to sting his eyes. He gave her a kiss on the forehead, then headed out to his car.

Just as he started up the car, his phone rang. It was that number he had seen earlier, so he picked up the phone and answered it.

"Hello."

"Hi, is this Jason Ryan?"

"Yes, it is. Who's asking?"

"It's me, Andrew Sullivan. We met when you were heading to Allerton."

"Ah, yes. How can I help you, Andrew?"

"Well, first, I need to be honest with you. I didn't realise who you were until my mom told me that my father had

married a lady from Allerton, Heather Gray, who is now Heather Stevens or Heather Ahns, I believe."

"That's true. Now all that is out in the open, where do we go from here?"

"Well, I haven't heard from my dad in a long time. I knew he was sick with heart issues, but then I heard he got better. It's been several years since he has been in touch with my mother. I was wondering, if you could help me find out where he might be?"

"I can talk to some of the Gray family to see what they know. I am only in town for a few days, but I will make sure to connect with them. I will call you back, at the number on my call display, if that is alright?"

"Thank you so much. Yes, the number on your display is my home number. Thanks, Jason."

"You're welcome. Talk to you soon."

"Bye."

Jason shook his head as he pulled out of the driveway. He would need to find a tactful way to talk to Elin about Andrew. Maybe his grandparents would be able to help him figure it all out. The drive back home was peaceful as the darkness was gentle and warm. He parked in the driveway, then saw his grandma look out the window. He climbed the stairs into the house where both his grandparents were sitting on the sofa, watching the evening news. They already had a cup of cocoa for him sitting near the recliner chair, with Scout sitting on the floor next to it. He watched some of the news until there was a commercial break, then they chatted about Rosa. They told him how excited they were to meet her. Feeling a little worn out, Jason excused himself and went up to his room. Tomorrow would be a better time to ask them about Andrew's situation.

His phone pinged as he got to his bedroom, it was Rosa saying good night. Smiling, he messaged her back, and they chatted for a few minutes. She couldn't believe how kind his family was to her. She told him that she adored his sister. Jason felt relieved that his family welcomed Rosa so warmly. There had been a few difficult years for the family, but having someone new join them now seemed like a very good thing. They ended their chat, then Jason got in his pj's. His muscles felt stiff from sitting still so long, but all he could muster was to get into bed; he was exhausted.

Thinking about his parents, he knew they would be at peace with how well things were going for him and Emma. He heard the grandparents turn off the TV as they headed to bed. Jason gently fell asleep.

Jason woke with a start, as Scout jumped up on the bed and cuddled up with him. It had been a long time since he had slept at home. He had forgotten about Scout's nightly routine. Jason smiled as he fell back asleep.

A constant loud beeping woke Jason from his sleep once again. It took a moment for him to realise that it was probably the alarm system. He headed into the hallway where he met his grandparents. They were both just waking up as well, so they slowly went downstairs to check on the alarm. Pictures on the alarm showed an attempted entry through the back door. Jason got his grandparents to stay by the phone as he made his way to the back door. The security light was blinking. Jason tried to see who it was by looking out the window. There didn't appear to be anyone there, so Jason got his grandpa to stay at the door when he went outside. Scout came barrelling out the door, barking at the gate to the backyard. He could hear the phone ringing and knew that it would be the alarm company. Just the other side of the backyard gate, Jason saw someone hiding behind a tree. With Scout by his side, he approached the person. Scout continued barking and lunging towards the figure. Jason asked who was there.

Sirens blared as the lights of a police car stopped out front of the house. Jason beckoned them to where he was standing. Scout sat at Jason's side as the officer approached the figure. The officer told them to stand up. They stood up slowly. Jason tried to see who it was, but it was too dark. The officer stood between him and the intruder. His grandpa came wandering over with a torch light. That is when Jason saw the intruder's face. It took him a moment to recognise him, then it clicked. It was Andrew, from the bus stop.

"Officer, I've met this person once before. His name is Andrew Sullivan."

"So, Andrew, what were you doing here tonight?"

"I was just looking for a place to sleep for the night. I thought maybe Jason would let me sleep here but all the lights were off, so I thought I could sneak in the back door. I swear that's all."

"Andrew, do you have any ID with you?"

"Yes, it's in my rucksack."

The officer reached inside the rucksack, bringing out a wallet with his ID. Then the officer called it in on his radio. It took several minutes for the radio to respond. Jason stood there watching Andrew's interaction with the officer. Too much had gone on in his life for him to vouch for someone he barely knew. This person certainly wouldn't be staying at the house. His grandpa had gone back inside and came out with his wallet.

"What's that for?" Jason asked.

"Well, I don't feel comfortable asking him to stay with us, but he can go to the hostel. I can supply the money for a room."

"Grandpa, I'm not sure…"

The officer's radio sputtered. Someone told them that there were no outstanding wants of warrants on the subject. With that, the officer looked at Andrew, then at Jason. He saw the grandfather holding out some money for Andrew.

"Officer, can you take Andrew to the hostel? We will pay the fee. Jason can meet up with him in the morning."

"Can do. Andrew, do you want to go to the hostel?"

"Sure, I guess. Can we chat in the morning, Jason?"

"We can arrange that. I will drop by the hostel around 10 am tomorrow, if that works for you?"

"Sure, thanks. Sorry about the hassle. I never thought it would go this far."

"It's okay. There is just a lot of history most people aren't aware of. Sleep well."

The officer took Andrew to the car so they could head to the hostel. Jason, Scout, and his grandparents went back inside. It was all quite unsettling, but Jason was determined not to let it bother him. Grandma had herbal tea all made up, so they sat for a while to chat about what had just happened. Soon they were all chatted out, so they reset the alarm, turned off the lights, and headed back to bed. Scout followed Jason into his room, jumping back on the bed. Jason lay awake for a while wondering what was going down with Andrew. He didn't feel that there was anything malicious in Andrew's arrival. Scout came up towards Jason's hand, so Jason gave him a pet. Having a dog was really a good idea. He could hardly wait to tell Emma about her dog's on-target reaction to the intruder.

Chapter Three

Emma woke to the sun shining through her curtains. She stretched a little before getting out of bed. Today was the day, graduation day. Prom was going to be amazing as she was going with Junior, Rosa, and Justin. She was so thankful that Junior was able to work everything out. She heard someone in the washroom and figured that Rosa had woken up before her. If her brother married Rosa, she would be happy. Her and Rosa had so many things in common from designing, to long walks, to caring for her brother.

Emma was sure that her mom and dad were smiling down on them all. Emma's first step each morning was often painful as her legs were immobile during the night, so she carefully put her feet on the carpet to lift herself up. The surgeons had promised that after the next set of surgeries, there would be little pain left. She eagerly looked forward to that.

As she opened her door Rosa left the washroom, so she quickly went in to get done with her morning routine. It only took a few minutes, but she slowed herself down to brush out her long hair, putting it back in a ponytail. Her mom used to love to brush her hair. Each time she made the ponytail she could remember her mom fixing her hair in pigtails. For special occasions, she would take Emma to the hairdresser to get it put into curls. That is what she wanted to do with her hair today. Her grandma had already made the appointment. The smell of breakfast drifted upstairs, adding to the fact that Emma was famished. When she started down the stairs, she heard Rosa's door open, so she waited for her at the top of the staircase.

"Good morning, Emma. Are you excited about your big day?"

"A little. And a little bit nervous, too."

"That's okay. To be honest with you, I'm a little nervous as well."

"Everyone will love you, Rosa. Just like Junior and I do."

"Oh, Emma. Thank you for that. I have grown pretty fond of both of you as well."

They stopped at the bottom of the stairs for Emma to give Rosa a hug. Then they found their way to that delicious aroma that was all around them. Grandma had made strawberry crepe roll ups. They grabbed a cup of coffee, then sat down at the table. Emma got up to take their plates to the stove where grandma was serving the crepes. Grandpa already had his food, but he looked up smiling. After all the trouble and sadness, it was almost unreal to be at such a place of peace with even a smidgen of joy.

Her grandma served her own food, then sat down with the rest of them to eat. As grandpa finished up his breakfast, the phone rang so he went to answer it, leaving the women to finish their breakfast. When he finished the phone call, he came back into the dining room and sat down again.

"That was Jason, he wanted to get in touch with you both, so I asked him to drop by. He is on his way. I think that is fair warning," he said with a grin.

Emma and Rosa smiled at grandpa, then quickly finished their food before they headed upstairs to prepare for the day. Emma took her prom dress down off the hanger as she looked to make sure it was all intact. It was incredibly beautiful. Emma smiled at all the times she and her mother had talked about what to wear. This would be her first self-designed formal dress that she had worn. Her lavender-tinged shoes set the dress off perfectly. The grandparents had rounded up some silver earrings and a beautiful amethyst necklace. The only things left were her nails, makeup, and hair. All of which she had appointments for this afternoon.

Rosa knocked as she entered her room. She looked at the young lady in front of her with the beautiful dress that she held in her arms. It almost made her cry. Jason had told her quite a bit about his parents and his family. She was amazed how they remained such kind people after all they had endured.

There was a knock at the downstairs door, so Emma put the dress back on the hanger as Rosa headed downstairs. Emma saw Ziggy on the bed, so she picked him up to go downstairs with her. He was Jason's cat after all, she knew Ziggy would be glad to see him. When Emma got downstairs, Rosa and Junior were chatting at the door. She decided to give them their privacy, so she went into the living room and looked out the window at the beautiful blue sky.

A few minutes later, they joined Emma in the living room. The grandparents were in the kitchen discussing the day. There would be a small dinner party tonight at the riverside cottage around 4 pm. Tomorrow the party would move to the Ryan house. The graduation ceremony would happen before the prom, starting at 6 pm. Everyone was starting to feel the excitement.

Ziggy decided he had been ignored for long enough, so he started to climb up Jason's leg to get to his lap. Once there, all anyone could hear was purring. Jason held Ziggy up and looked him in the eyes. For whatever reason, their bond was still intact. Jason looked around Ziggy, to Rosa and Emma.

"Well, you guys look like you are ready for the day. Rosa, you said you wanted to look around for something to wear for tonight, so we can do that this morning. I just have one small thing to take care of before that."

"Thanks, Jason. Can I help you with whatever you need to do?"

"You know what, you probably can. It's a bit of a long story but I met this young guy when I was heading this way. We exchanged phone information when I talked to him yesterday. However, last night he came to our house and tried to enter as he was looking for a place to sleep. The police were called but no charges were laid. Grandpa paid for him to stay at the hostel. Now, I need to go figure out what to make of all this. You are more than welcome to come, Rosa, if you still want to."

"It might be helpful to have another person there, Jason. I would like to help if I can."

"I will take you up on that, but you need to get ready cause I told him I'd pick him up at the hostel at 10 am. That gives us 15 minutes."

Rosa headed upstairs to get her shoes while Emma and Jason chatted a little more. Jason went over to Emma to give her a hug. Even with the grandparents being close by, sometimes it felt like it was just them against the world. Ziggy cuddled on Jason's shoulder then scuttled under his jacket as the grandparents came into the room. They both gave Jason a hug. He was feeling like he had been on an emotional roller coaster for the better part of the week. With year end finals and Emma's graduation, he was probably pushing too hard to stay focused. The intruder last night didn't help much either, but Jason was determined to keep everything in its proper place. Andrew could hardly be compared to the harassment that his family had been through. It was probably just that he was missing their mom and dad.

When Rosa came back downstairs, Jason and Rosa headed out to meet with Andrew. Emma decided to take a minute or two to text Justin. She was glad he was going to be her 'date', but she also understood her grandparents' reluctance. Justin was a good soul. They talked a lot about their families. Often, they would talk about what their folks would say if they knew they were good friends. However, both were aware that Emma had things to take care of before getting serious with anyone. Within a couple minutes, Justin had messaged her back. He was happy about going with Emma to the prom. He told her that Elin helped with that.

Emma had always liked Elin, even if they didn't know each other extremely well. Junior had lived with Elin's family for a while after their dad died. Everything was so messed up at that time and she was just beginning to walk again. Her mom's parents had taken her in, while the other grandparents had stayed in the house with Scout, paying rent of all things. Dying without a will, set up a bizarre set of circumstances.

"Emma, it's time to head to the hairdresser," her grandma called.

"Be right there," she replied as she grabbed a jacket.

Her grandma met her at the bottom of the stairs as they headed out to the car.

It was getting late when Emma finished with the hairdresser and the cosmetician. Her hair, nails and makeup were done. It was time to head home for their dinner party. Grandma was so organised about all of this. Emma realised that her grandma was skilled at many things. She had made the past few years bearable, as she missed her mother intensely. A car pulled out in front of them and honked. It took Emma a minute to realise it was Junior. It looked like they were heading towards the cottage as well.

Jason had left Andrew at the hostel, telling him they could talk more tomorrow. He didn't want to say anything about Emma's prom, as he was still uncertain about Andrew's motivation. He and Rosa talked a little after dropping Andrew off. Together they had designed a plan for the upcoming couple of days. Jason was going to talk to Elin about Heather's ex-husband. Losing a father is something that Jason could sympathise with. He would see Elin when they picked up Justin for the prom, so maybe he could set up a time to talk then. Hopefully, he wouldn't be adding any pain to a situation that he knew nothing about.

Both cars pulled into the driveway at the same time and Rosa got out. She took a few packages from the backseat of the car. She had found a dress and shoes at one of the local shops. Jason had bought her a necklace to go with it. Being with Jason today was fun. Rosa saw him in a different way as he dealt with the people of his hometown. They all went inside to dress for dinner as quite soon after dinner, they would need to leave to get Emma to her graduation on time.

The dinner was amazing with everyone in their party outfits. Emma was incredibly beautiful all made up. Her grandparents glowed as they watched her take her first steps into the adult world. She always did adult well, anyway. They supposed, it was because of coming out of great tragedy that she became such an amazing young woman. Her parents would have been immensely proud of her. Jason had to stop thinking of the past in order to not end up sobbing. He got up from the table and looked out at the river. He could see a couple of seals out there. When he turned around, he saw that Emma was behind him watching them as well. Giving her a hug, Jason excused himself then sat back down at the table. Being home felt good but it wasn't always easy.

When everyone had finished eating, Jason and Rosa helped to collect the dishes to take them to the kitchen. The grandparents made some coffee and brought out some sweets, but the young people were getting anxious. Jason excused the three of them, telling the grandparents they were going to go for a short drive before the graduation ceremony. They hopped into Jason's car and headed out. After 15 minutes or so, Jason drove into Elin's driveway. He asked Rosa to come with him to meet Elin. He had told her a little about staying with Elin when his dad died. They made it to the front door as Elin opened it.

"Jason, so good to see you. Who is this beautiful lady with you?"

"Elin, this is Rosa. Rosa, this is Elin. You are two of my favourite young women."

"Ah, Jason, you are sweet. Unfortunately, I am not that young anymore, at least I don't feel that way."

"It's good to meet you, Elin. Jason has told me a lot about you."

"Oh, yah. Good, I hope. Jason has told me absolutely nothing about you, but then it always was hard to get Jason to talk."

"Elin, we talked a lot when I lived here. Just life and school seem to keep me busy. I hear you are going to be at the prom as well. Maybe we will get a chance to chat, if not, there is a few things I would like to talk to you about. Could you meet with me, or us, tomorrow some time?"

"For sure. It sounds serious. Hope everything is going well."

"It is just something that has come up in the last couple of days. Nothing too big."

"OK. How about 10 am tomorrow, we can meet here at my place?"

"Sounds good, Elin. We'll be here at 10 am."

"Justin, Emma's ride is waiting for you," Elin called into the house.

"Coming…" Justin replied as he appeared in the doorway. He looked so grown up in his suit that Elin almost gasped. He carried a container with a wrist corsage in pink and deep purple. She moved out of the door to let him through as he headed to the car to give Emma her corsage.

"I'll meet you all at the graduation ceremony, save me a seat. I have been asked to help with the prom. I must remember to bring my camera."

As Jason headed out onto the motorway to go to the school, he did a double take. Walking along the motorway was Andrew. Jason slowed down, pulling over so that Rosa could ask Andrew where he was going. He told her he was heading to a local restaurant just around the corner. Jason told him that they have a meeting with Elin tomorrow at 10 am and Andrew grinned. They left him at that point as they were running out of time to get to the graduation. Emma looked out the window at the young man, but she didn't know him. However, Justin fiddled with his hands as they took off down the road. They pulled into the school car park. Jason let the ladies and Justin out at the door to the auditorium. He quickly parked the car, then headed into the building.

Jason was glad that Rosa was with the two younger people, as he noticed the way that Justin acted when they were talking with Andrew. He felt that Justin may know Andrew or at least know about him. This was turning out to be an interesting evening, but Jason promised himself he would not let Emma out of his sight. She was his number one concern, and he was thankful that Rosa was here with him. It would make the task that much less daunting.

Some of Jason's teachers came up to him to shake his hand. They were curious to know how his studies were going and they grinned when he told them he was just finishing his engineering degree. Justin guided Emma to the refreshment table where they grabbed a glass of punch. Rosa followed them as the teachers continued to gather around Jason. They found seats, saving a seat for Jason and the grandparents as the music to begin the graduation ceremony started. Jason found them, then got up to guide the grandparents to where they were sitting.

When they called Emma's name, Jason watched her climb the three stairs and walk across the stage. There was barely a noticeable limp, but Jason knew the challenging work it took for Emma to have progressed this far. They presented her with her diploma. As she started to head down the stairs they called her back, giving her the exclusive title of being this year's recipient of the Comeback Award. She turned back to the presenter with tears pouring down her face. Elin jockeyed to the front of the ceremony to take her picture. With the award, came a five-thousand-dollar scholarship for post-secondary education. They asked her to say a few words. She stood silent for a minute, then looked out at Jason in the crowd.

"Sometimes life can throw you a curve ball that seems to hit you so hard you can barely breathe. However, when I look out at the crowd, I see the people who have walked through this past several years with me. My brother, Jason, and my grandparents have walked with me through some of the darkest days I have known. They picked me up when I stumbled, literally. They hugged me when the world seemed to be closing in on me. Somehow, we made it here, today. I have family and friends, teachers and medical teams who walked alongside me as my body healed and I was able to walk once again. None of this would have been possible without each one of you."

The gym roared with applause as Emma went back to her seat. Jason was looking down at the floor trying to hold back the sobs, so Emma gave him a kiss on the forehead and a hug. It was the Ryan duplex that only he and Emma understood. He stood up to hug her. They continued with the ceremony as Jason and Emma took their seats. The grandparents dried their eyes as they smiled at Emma. She had come so far and could now chart her own course from here on. Elin held Justin's hand. He smiled because he knew how much Emma had overcome. They each had their journeys to complete but even today he knew that he loved Emma very much and he would wait for her.

The graduation ceremony wrapped up as the parents took pictures with their grads. Then it was time to start the prom. The parents headed home as the students headed to the gym that had been transformed by its decorators into a panacea of European destinations. Jason remembered his graduation just after his father had passed on. The emotions threatened to overwhelm him. Emma grabbed him by the hand, they had the first dance together. Rosa and Justin watched as the two of them glided along the floor. When the dance ended, Jason came back to where Rosa was standing. Emma took Justin's hand as they headed out onto the dance floor. Rosa tucked her hand in Jason's hand and gave him a hug. In so many ways, this was the crossroads where the past would be left behind, where their futures could begin.

Elin came over to Rosa and Jason as they watched the young people dance their night away. Once in a while, Emma came back to sit for a while, then Justin would dance with Elin or Rosa. For the last song, Jason took Rosa's hand

and headed onto the dance floor. Every graduation ended with the same song. Yes, they were looking forward to the time of their lives. Jason had to smile at how seamlessly Rosa fit into his family and community. He knew his parents would be pleased, especially tonight of all nights. As they all came back together after the last dance, Emma and Elin decided it was time to go to the washroom before heading home. There was a bit of a wait, so they chatted about the future.

When they finally got to the washroom, it was almost empty. There was a rucksack sitting against the wall, so Elin picked it up and asked if it belonged to anyone in the washroom. There was no reply. Gently she opened it to see if there was a name in it. She quickly closed it back up when she saw a gun in the bag as well as a bunch of photos. She took it to the teacher in charge as they all headed home. Just as they reached their cars, Elin's phone rang. Jason, Rosa, and Emma got in their car but waited until Elin was finished on the phone. When Elin got off the phone, she looked a little upset, but they said their goodbyes. Elin and Justin got in her car and headed out.

Back at the riverside cottage, Rosa and Emma got out of the car. Jason gave them each a hug, then got back in his car. He thought about this night and felt that things were on the right track. Just as he pulled into his driveway, his phone rang.

"Hello," he answered.

"Jason, it's Elin. I just thought I should let you know that the rucksack Emma and I found in the washroom had a gun in it as well as photos. The gun was enough to stop me from looking any further, but the school chaperon called to tell me some of the pictures were of my sister."

"Oh. That is odd. The person we are going to meet with tomorrow claims to be the son of Heather's husband. He didn't have a gun, but I know that he wanted to ask about Heather's husband as he was looking for his dad."

"Do you think it's safe to meet with him?"

"Hmmm. Maybe at a café rather than at your place. Meet me at the coffee shop at 9:30 am. I will tell him to join us for 10 am."

"Sounds good. I know that the school chaperon was turning it all over to the police. See you tomorrow morning."

Jason decided to head to the hostel to see if he could find Andrew. As he pulled up to the hostel building, Jason saw Andrew lounging outside. It was a little late to be outside, but it was still warm. When Jason pulled into the car park, Andrew headed over to his car. Usually, Jason could read people well, but Andrew just seemed to be a lost kid, nothing more and nothing less.

"Hey Andrew, how has your day gone?"

"Pretty good. And you?"

"Good, my sister just graduated so we were at the school tonight. It's a big deal as she has had so many things to derail her and through it all she made it anyway."

"Wow. Are we still on for tomorrow morning?"

"Yup. We are going to meet at the coffee shop, just across the road and up a block. Can you meet us there about 10 am?"

"No problem. Why the change of meeting place?"

"Just a convenience thing. Is that okay with you?"

“Sure, I will meet you there at 10 am.”

“Well, I’d better get home, today has been pretty busy and I’m a little tired.”

“Rest well. See you tomorrow.”

At that, Jason started his car and headed home.

Chapter Four

Emma woke with a start. Her bed was shaking and there was a small rumble coming from somewhere. She looked out her window where she saw the trees shaking a little. Then it clicked, they were having a small earthquake. It had been years since they had felt a quake, but it was an occurrence that you never forget. Getting out of bed, she put on her slippers and robe. The shaking ceased as Emma opened her bedroom door. Living on the island, everyone practiced earthquake drills in school. When Emma was halfway down the stairs, Rosa came out of her bedroom. She knocked on Emma's door.

"I'm heading downstairs, Rosa. It's important to head to the main floor. I can hear grandma and grandpa in the kitchen. They have the TV on in the living room."

"What's going on, Emma? Is this what the west coasters call a 'shaker'?"

"For sure. There will be a warning if a tidal wave or tsunami builds. It usually has to be a pretty strong quake to make a tidal wave."

"Would this be considered a strong quake?"

"I'm not sure. We will get warnings on the TV. There is also a tsunami warning siren that goes off if a wave is building."

"Hey, Grandma, that was an earthquake, right?"

"Yes, dear, but the reports say it wasn't big enough to cause a tidal wave."

"Phew. Thank goodness. It has been a few years since we have had an earthquake. Have you heard anything on the news?"

"Not much, just that there was an earthquake about 15 km off the coast. First reports say it was a 4.2. An all-clear hasn't been issued yet, but it seems kind of small to cause a tidal wave."

Rosa and Emma grabbed a cup of coffee as they sat down at the kitchen table. Grandpa came in from the living room to sit down with them. He looked a little tired. Emma knew that those who had lived on the island for a long while still had memories of the last tidal wave. It was one of the reasons her mother's parents had moved to the mainland. However, the island had a way of coaxing people to move back. There was nowhere else Emma wanted to live, the mountains, rivers and people were unique. Emma thought her mom's parents would probably move back to the mainland soon, but they hadn't said too much so far.

Ziggy came out from under the table, meowing. Emma bent down to pick him up and he just clung to her. It must be scary to be so small when something like this happened. Grandma was already working on breakfast. They each served themselves, then ate in relative quiet. The TV was stating that there was no tsunami expected, so everyone let out a sigh of relief. Ziggy climbed up Emma's robe, settling on her shoulder like an infant. Table etiquette didn't allow cats at the table, but the grandparents didn't make her put him down. The phone rang. Somehow, she knew it would be Junior, checking to make sure they were all okay. Grandma got up to answer the phone. They could hear her telling Junior they were all fine. Then she called Rosa to the phone, Jason wanted to talk with her.

"Hey, Rosa, how are you doing? I know you aren't familiar with earthquakes, but from what has been announced, there will be no tidal wave. But there is a possibility of after-shocks so don't let them frighten you."

"I'm good, Jason. Are we still meeting Elin and Andrew this morning?"

"Yes, I talked with Andrew on my way home last night. He will meet us at the coffee shop at 10 am. I asked Elin to be there at 9:30 am so we can get settled before Andrew shows up. The gun has got Elin really freaked out."

"It is kind of scary, especially with the pictures of her sister. It makes it that much more concerning."

"That's true. We aren't sure the rucksack belongs to Andrew, but it is sort of a coincidence."

"It is. Did the rucksack match what Andrew had when he showed up at your place?"

"I didn't see the one at the school but that is something we can discuss before Andrew shows up."

"What time will you be picking me up?"

"In half an hour, if that works for you?"

"I'll make it work. See you soon."

Rosa hung up then went back to the kitchen to finish her breakfast. She ate quickly then went upstairs to get dressed as time was ticking by quickly. She just put on jeans and a shirt as she was saving her other outfit for the party this afternoon. There she would meet a lot of family and family friends that she hadn't met last night. She was a little nervous but so far it had been a positive experience. She really liked Jason's family. As she pulled her hair into a ponytail, she heard a light honk coming from downstairs. She grabbed her jacket and wallet as she headed downstairs. After thanking Emma's grandparents for the delicious breakfast, she headed outside to Jason's car.

They headed for the café, then noticed they had 15 minutes to fill so they took a quick drive down by the river. The morning sun was beautiful against the mountains. Rosa could see why Jason loved this place so much. She was used to a more metropolitan lifestyle but it's amazing what could be conquered by being in love with someone. It was time to meet Elin, so they headed to the café. Elin had just arrived when they got there. Once inside they got a table, ordered coffee, and began to discuss what they would be looking for when they met with Andrew. By the time 10 am hit, they had it all figured out. They looked forward to Andrew joining them.

By 10:15 am, Jason was starting to wonder what had happened to Andrew. By 10:30 am, Jason decided to drive to the hostel to find him. An outreach worker was waiting by the door, talking with the people as they left. Jason watched him for a while, then headed his way.

"Hi, I was supposed to meet Andrew Sullivan for breakfast this morning, but he didn't show up. Is he still sleeping?"

"I'll go check."

Jason waited until the outreach worker came back outside.

"He's not here right now. He may have gone into town earlier, but no one seems to know for sure."

"OK, thanks."

Jason made his way back to the café, watching carefully for any sign of Andrew. Things like this still made Jason feel a little anxious. It was too easy to think back before his mother died. He would never tolerate anyone threatening his family again, so he took a quick trip by the police station to make an inquiry. He was met at the door by an officer who was just on his way out to patrol.

"Hi, sorry to bother you, but I was just wondering if you had any contact with someone called Andrew Sullivan?"

"Why are you asking?" the officer replied.

"Well, it's a long story, but I was supposed to meet Andrew for breakfast at 10 am and he never showed. He had been staying at the hostel."

"How well do you know Mr. Sullivan?"

"We met a couple days ago. He ended up coming to my house the next night, in fact the police were called for that."

"Oh. So would you be Austin Ryan?"

"No, that's my grandfather. Why?"

"That was the name on the report. We found Andrew after the quake this morning. He got slightly injured during the shaking, so he was taken to the hospital. He may still be there."

"Thank you, officer, I will head up there to see."

"Let me call. It could save you a trip."

"Thanks."

The officer dialled a number and waited a couple seconds. Then he asked about the young man they had brought in earlier. He wrote down something, then ended the call.

"Mr. Sullivan was released about half an hour ago, into his mother's care."

"Ok. Thanks. Glad he's okay."

Jason left and headed back to the café. The two women had ordered another round of coffee. When he came in the door, he realised he had been gone longer than they expected.

"Did you find Andrew?" Rosa asked.

"Not exactly. He got slightly injured during the earthquake. He was taken to the hospital. Apparently, his mother picked him up from there."

"OK, that makes sense," Elin added.

"Yup, however, we will probably hear from him again."

"Why do you think that?" Elin asked.

"He seemed to be set on finding out more about his dad. That may motivate him to contact us again. I think I will give him a call tomorrow to see how he's doing."

"Sounds good, I will be heading back to the university tomorrow. When do you head back, Jason?" Rosa said.

"Probably tomorrow but I'm thinking about spending the summer break here. I've missed it."

"I understand why, it's beautiful here. Plus, you have lots of friends and family that still lives here."

"It also seems to bring about a peace, at least in me."

They finished their coffee then Rosa and Jason headed home. Rosa had to do her makeup before getting dressed for the party. Jason knew he was needed to help set up for the party. Elin would be at the party as well. Rosa felt like she was starting to understand a bit more about Jason's family and friends.

Jason drove into his driveway then hustled upstairs to help the grandparents decorate. He was surprised at the way things all went together. This party was important, he was proud of Emma, scholastically and personally. It wasn't an easy road for her, but she had graduated with honours. She deserved any fuss they could make over her. Scout was smart. He had decided to stay at the top of the staircase leading up to the washroom. After a bit, he headed for the back door. Jason thought he should let Scout out so he could get a little exercise before the party. Hopefully, he would sleep right through it, but Jason wasn't putting any bets on that.

Grandma was in the kitchen making all sorts of foods, from snacks to tacos, to dessert bars and fruit punch. He wished that his mom and dad could be here to see all of this, but he knew that they would approve. The grandparents were utterly amazing, but on a night like tonight it would have been great to have their parents around. Once the decorations were all up, Jason asked if he could help with anything else. The grandparents told him to go rest until the party. Scout had been barking outside, so grandpa went out back to let him in.

Jason laid down on his bed. It seemed like only minutes later, the doorbell rang. Jason looked at his alarm clock. He saw that it was time to get dressed, it was party time. His grandpa came up the stairs to tell him that Rosa, Emma, and Alison's parents had arrived. Jason just had to get his shoes and socks on. As he finished in the washroom, the doorbell rang again. He quickly headed downstairs. Elin and Justin were coming into the living room, so Jason gave Justin a high five and a hug for Elin. For whatever reason, he really did feel festive even after what had happened with Andrew. Grandma Iris was busily putting the food out on the long table in the living room, so Jason grabbed a couple of the food trays as he made his way to the long table. Emma was totally stunning in a dark green skirt and tan print blouse. Jason looked around at those gathered in the room, wondering how the years had passed so quickly.

Scout started getting a little rambunctious, so Grandpa Austin took him back out so he could run off some of his energy. Jason brought out his food dishes so Scout could have his dinner in peace. The two of them took a moment to look at the sky. It was a moment of stillness in a remarkably busy world. Grandma shouted at them to come on inside, she needed help with the punch bowl and cake. Both Austin and Jason quickly walked to the back door, gave each other a grin, then started being the party hosts. They looked back to see that Scout was lying in his doghouse.

"You know, we will probably need to bring him back in soon, especially if he starts howling."

"Just give me a nudge, Grandpa, when you feel he needs to come in."

As they got into the kitchen, grandma gave Jason the punch bowl while Austin got the cake. She had made the cake herself; it was beautiful! They headed into the living room to put the items down as the doorbell rang again. It was Casey, Raymond, Melanie and her mother so Jason went to the door to usher them in. Jason's uncle and aunt were the next people to arrive. They immediately started helping Iris with the food and other items, which gave Jason time to mingle a little. He wondered if his mother's sisters and brother would be coming tonight, he hoped so, it would mean so much to Emma and the grandparents.

Jason stayed near the door to greet the people who were continuing to arrive. He had forgotten how many they had invited. He was glad he and grandpa had moved most of the furniture upstairs as well as putting out a bunch of chairs. Daniel and Heather came to the door, so Jason greeted them as he ushered them in.

"Junior, so good to see you. This looks like the best party in town," Daniel stated.

"I don't know about the best, but definitely well-attended," Jason replied.

"Can you show us the way to Emma?"

"She's right over there near the punch bowl. That is her designated place, according to the grandmas," Jason replied.

They each gave Jason a nod and moved towards the punch bowl. The pastor from the church down the road as well as several church members were the next ones to come to the door. Jason greeted each of them. The pastor smiled at Jason.

"Do you want me to bless the food, Jason?"

Jason looked down at the floor as the pastor gave him a side hug.

"Just teasing, Jason. You have an amazing family."

"Thanks, Pastor," Jason replied. "I guess I will never outgrow the blessing the food remark, but that's okay. It brings back some pretty amazing memories of our dad."

"You know how proud he would be of you and Emma?"

"I hope it makes him and mom smile. It almost feels like they are with us today."

"Keep on doing what you're doing, Jason. Each accomplishment is a testimony to your recovery. You will be graduating in December, won't you?"

"Yes, that's the plan. Thanks, Pastor, for coming to celebrate Emma's graduation," Jason said as the pastor moved into the room.

Some of Emma's friends from school came in next. They had been practicing some music that they wanted to share with them all. Jason found them chairs, then the room noise came down to a whisper. The young women started with his dad's favourite song about grace and freedom. Iris and Austin stepped into the kitchen. Jason saw the start of tears in their eyes. The next song was Emma's favourite, it was an old classic about moving on and growing up. By the end of the song, the grandparents were back in the room.

Emma could hear Scout barking outside so she decided it would be a suitable time to take a break and see how Scout was doing. As she walked outside, the sunshine fell against her, she felt a moment of relaxation. She looked over at Scout as he was standing at the door to his kennel, barking. Emma looked around her but couldn't see anyone or anything that would be upsetting Scout, so she made her way over to his run. Just as she passed by the garden shed, she felt something slam against the back of her legs. She went flying to the ground. As she tried to get herself upright again, she heard someone go running through the garden and over the fence. Scout was barking louder and louder as Emma tried to get up from the ground. The pain was starting to increase so she gently rolled herself over to a sitting position. There was no blood on her legs or her skirt, so she knew the blow didn't cause an open wound.

Not wanting to cause a disturbance, Emma butt-scooted over to Scout's run as she attempted to pull herself to her feet. Scout started to lick her hands. Emma felt the tears well up in her eyes. She hadn't told anyone that she was heading outside. She wondered how long it would take for someone to notice she wasn't there. She stayed sitting with Scout watching over her until finally she heard the back door open. Grandma Iris looked out over the backyard and saw that Emma was sitting near the dog run. Calling for grandpa, her grandma made her way over to Emma.

"Emma, are you OK?"

"Not really," Emma replied. "I heard Scout barking and came out to see why. Someone hit me on the back of the legs. I ended up on the grass. They took off running through the garden. The security cameras may have caught a picture of whoever it was, but I never saw who it was."

"Austin, I need your help here!" her grandma called out.

Austin and Jason came to the back door. They saw Emma with her grandma near the dog run, so they headed towards them. Emma tried to make herself stand but with no luck. Jason reached Emma, asking her what had happened.

"I went out to see why Scout was barking. Someone hit me from behind. I can't seem to get myself to stand up, but there is no blood, so no wounds."

"Do you want us to help you up?" Austin asked.

"Let's give it a try," Emma responded.

Austin stood on one side of Emma while Jason was on the other side. They put their shoulders under her arms as they slowly tried to raise her up. Emma didn't want to ruin the celebration, so she walked with them to the back door. The steps were a new challenge. By then, they knew that she needed medical attention. With the three of them half-carrying her into the house, Austin got a chair, telling her to sit down for a minute. Her skirt was a little wrinkled but was relatively clean, so they walked her into the living room. Everyone took a deep breath when they saw her. The pastor came over to her to ask if they needed him to call an ambulance.

Jason took a moment to talk to their gathered guests to tell them Emma had a fall out back. He didn't go any further as it would have just added more speculation. After thanking them for attending, he told them that Emma needed to see a doctor so she would have to be leaving soon. The guests came to speak to Emma and give her a hug as they left. The pastor had already placed a call to the ambulance station. Within ten minutes, the paramedics appeared at the door. They did their initial diagnosis but decided it would be prudent for her to seek medical attention at the hospital. Grabbing a stretcher from their ambulance, they gently placed Emma on it, then wheeled her down the ramp.

Rosa held Jason's hand as she saw the concern etched onto his face. She knew there must be more than what he had told the guests, but she was smart enough to let it go for now. The grandparents had started to clear off the table, so Rosa and Jason began doing the same. They were discussing who would go to the hospital. In the final decision, it was decided they all would go. It was important that Emma knew they were there for her.

Emma dreaded the thought of heading to the hospital. She had enough of hospital life to do her a lifetime. Yet, she knew that something wasn't working well, so she sat quietly as they drove into the emergency bay. The paramedics got out of the vehicle and pushed the stretcher into the hospital, updating her chart as they continued to the nurses' station. Her family doctor met her in the ER. He asked her a ton of questions until Emma was done. She was tired, scared and a little anxious so they took her into an ER room to give her a few minutes to rest. Her doctor ordered x-rays for her legs; plus, a relaxant to help her through this stage.

The doctor asked the ambulance attendants more questions until they were called away for another call. As the ambulance pulled away, the grandparents and Jason pulled into the parking area. They knew it would seem a little weird for them all to go in, so it was decided that Jason and Iris would go in first. At the nurses' station they were told that she had just been put in room seven, and a couple of them could go in and visit at a time. Jason and Iris went looking for the room. Looking into the room they saw that Emma was lying peacefully on the bed, the meds had already kicked in. Emma clenched onto Iris' hand and wouldn't let it go. It all felt too familiar. She wasn't willing to stay in the hospital, not even for a day.

The paramedics had informed the police about the incident. As Jason and Iris sat with Emma, an officer came to the door to ask her some questions. Emma gave the officer what she could remember, but she really didn't see anybody when she went outside. The officer wrote down what she told him, then went to the nurses' station for the description of her injuries. A brief time later, the x-ray technician came into Emma's room. They asked Jason and Iris to leave for a few minutes. Iris and Jason decided it was a suitable time to go back to the others to tell them what they knew. They decided that Austin and Rosa would be the next ones to visit, then the other grandparents.

As Rosa and Austin entered the room, Emma dried the tears from her eyes. Apparently, the x-ray didn't look too bad, but the technician said her doctor would be in to see her shortly. Emma was hoping they would let her go home, but trying to get up the stairs anywhere would be difficult. As the ramp was still up at the Ryan's family house, Emma felt they might let her go home if she stayed there.

The next thing would be to find a wheelchair, so Austin got Jason to see where they could rent one. Jason started looking online as the time slipped away. His grandma went to the hospital coffee shop, to grab coffee for them all. He found two places where they could rent a wheelchair. He got one of the places to put a hold on one by paying them online. Now, Emma just had to be all right.

Chapter Five

The doctor did a group of tests on Emma, then let her family know that the damage to her leg was minimal, but she would need to avoid over-exertion. While they were waiting, the family had decided on an action plan in case Emma needed extra support. They were going to move her to the family home as there was a ramp and a stair lift. Ziggy would travel back there with her, which would give Alison's parents a chance to rest a little.

Jason had already called the university to let them know what had happened. He had been granted extra days away from his programme. However, they would expect him to do his remaining assignments during this time. It was a good thing that Jason had come to town with his computer, as all his assignments were on it. Rosa would be going back to class, but she told him that if he needed her for anything, she would come back.

Elin and Justin showed up at the hospital to ask about Emma. Jason told them she was having trouble with one of her legs, so she would be moving to the Ryan's family house. Justin seemed a little uneasy, so Elin decided it was time to go home. Obviously, something was bothering him. She took the long route home, past the marina and along the river. A slight drizzle was coming down, but it was warm. Justin watched the passing vehicles, feeling like he was going to explode. He had already figured out who had hit Emma. He knew that somehow, he had to protect her. They pulled into their driveway, but Justin waited for Elin to unlock the house.

Once inside the house, Elin took him by the shoulders and faced him towards her.

"What's going on, Justin? And don't tell me nothing."

"What do you mean?"

"Something is going on. You are all tensed up, you've been that way since we left the Ryan house."

"I'm just concerned about Emma. That is all, I swear."

"You know, it's never smart to lie to me. I can see a lie coming a mile away."

"I'm not lying. I AM concerned about Emma."

"Fair enough. We're both concerned about Emma, but there is something else. It would be best to spit it out now."

"I'm tired. I just want to go get into comfortable clothes and lie down for a bit."

Elin let go of him, so he sauntered off to his bedroom. Once he was there, he sat down on the bed. How did this happen when he was sure that Andrew was at home with his mother? First there was the rucksack at the school, now this. What was the point of hurting Emma? Andrew had told Justin about meeting up with Jason, and Justin knew that was not going to end well. Andrew had also threatened to go to Justin's mother to ask the questions that he had been wanting to ask. Justin had talked him out of that, but now, they were at this point. Either Justin needed to tell Elin about Andrew, or he would talk to Jason. Hopefully, they could stop any further damage.

Justin got into his jeans and a t-shirt then looked out his bedroom window. Things had been good since staying with the Gray family. He and Daniel, Elin's brother, got along well. In fact, Daniel wanted to mentor him, to have Justin join his financial management business. It had always been easy to talk with Daniel, so Justin picked up his phone to make the call. Daniel was still on his way back to the southern tip of the island, so the call went to voicemail. Justin left him a message to call him when he was able to do so. His phone dinged, there was a message from Emma. She was out of the hospital and in the process of moving to the Ryan's family home. That would make it easier for her to move around, but Justin had a deep foreboding about the move. It all seemed a little too much like déjà vu.

Elin knocked on Justin's door, so he gently opened it.

"Justin, I'm sorry if I was too blunt when we talked. I just have this sinking feeling that something is going on that I don't, and should, know about."

"There is something. I called Daniel to talk with him, but it went to voicemail."

Elin looked out the window as Daniel's car pulled into the driveway. She turned around. Justin was trying so hard to be strong, but he was starting to break down.

"Daniel just drove into the driveway. I think all of us are a little spooked by what went down at Emma's party. Your message may have gotten Daniel to turn around, but it could be he felt the intensity of what happened to Emma. Either way, you can talk to both Daniel and me, or I can go for a drive while you and Daniel talk."

"Elin, don't get me wrong, I know I can trust you, but it just feels like things are about to explode. You are welcome to be part of the conversation. Just don't be surprised at what you hear."

Daniel came into the house. They could hear him in the hallway. He stopped at the washroom, so Elin gave Justin a hug. Whatever happened, they were family. They heard Daniel continue down the hall and stop at Justin's room. He looked in at Justin and Elin then raised his eyebrows.

"What's going on? I just listened to Justin's message. Let's go and have a coffee. We need to talk this through."

"Sounds good," Elin replied.

Elin put the coffee on. They sat at the table, looking at each other, none of them wanting to start the conversation. Elin got up to get some mugs. Justin looked down at the table. He saw Fancy lying at their feet. She looked at Justin, wagging her tail. She seemed to know something was going down. Elin called Fancy as she put out her food.

Daniel looked over at Justin. He could see Justin was struggling with something. Elin picked up Fancy to carry her to where they were sitting. Fancy wagged her tail so hard it was funny. Elin grinned at Fancy then Daniel couldn't help but giggle as well. His giggle was infamous. He had been teased a lot about it when he was a kid. Justin looked over at them.

Fancy popped down onto the floor and went over to Justin. She looked up at him with those big, brown eyes. It was impossible to miss the look, so Justin picked her up. Fancy gave his face a good licking.

"Well, I'll start," Daniel said. "Justin, you left me a message to call you back. Is something going on that we should know?"

Justin glanced down at Fancy on his lap and gave her a pet. He had to find the right words.

"There is something that I have found out, that could be harming people I care about."

"That sounds a little vague, Justin. Could you give us a little more of the details?" Elin asked.

"You know that guy, Andrew, who you and Jason were going to meet. He wasn't totally honest with Jason."

"From what Jason told me, he believes that Andrew is the son of Heather's ex-husband. Is that part, correct?"

"It's a possibility but not a probability. Andrew thinks his mom lied to him and that his father was my father."

"Wow. That is a substantial change. How are you doing with that?"

"I don't know, a part of me doesn't want to know. Andrew wanted to talk with my mother, but she is in a fragile state. I was afraid it would push her over the edge. So, he decided to go the other route and search out Heather's ex."

Daniel sat back in his chair to think about how to proceed with this. Were Jason and Emma in harm's way? Would Andrew cause them grief or was he just trying to figure this all out? Looking around the table, Daniel took his mobile phone out to call his sister, Heather.

"Daniel, we haven't talked in ages. Is everything OK?" Heather said as she answered her phone.

"It's been a while, we sure miss having you around. How are things going on the mainland?"

"Things are going really well. Roy and I have had a couple meals together, now that he is recovered from his heart surgery. I love working at the designer's factory. I am hoping to spend a couple weeks with you this summer."

"Gosh, slow down a little, Heather. We need to talk more often. I need your help with a situation here."

"What's that?"

"There is a young fellow here who thinks that Roy may be his father. That is a big maybe, but it is stirring up a lot of uncertainty in this neck of the woods."

"Oh. I don't know of any kids, but I could bring it up with him."

"Only if you feel OK doing this. The other possibility is that, the young person is a stepbrother to Justin here. It's getting important to find out whatever we can. Things are starting to get overheated here. There has been at least one injury, maybe two, that may have happened because of this. Do you think you could ask Roy about this?"

"Yes. I'll do that as soon as we hang up."

"Thanks, Heather. Let us know when you find out. Love you, kiddo."

"Love you, too."

Daniel put down his phone and looked over at Justin. He could see the tension lessen, then Justin let the tears flow. Elin got up to give him a hug as Fancy laid her head on his shoulder. The next part would be unpopular, but it needed to happen.

"Justin, did Andrew hurt Emma? Was it him that hit her from behind?"

"It's possible. I haven't had a chance to talk with him yet."

Daniel got up to get the handset from the home phone. He gave it to Justin.

"Call him and find out, please."

Justin made the call then waited for Andrew to answer. He was going to hang up when Andrew answered the phone.

"Hey, Justin. What's up?"

"Not too much. How are you feeling after your injury?"

"Pretty good, just sprained my ankle a little; plus, a small fracture in the bone near my toes."

"Good to hear you are doing OK. I've been wondering ever since I heard you were taken back home by your mom."

"Yes, that's another matter. I'm in your fair city now, do you want to hang out later?"

"I'm pretty tired. Do you have a place to stay?"

"I thought I would ask Jason if I could stay with them, but that isn't likely."

"It would be better just to stay away from that one."

"You don't say. How about me staying with you?"

"I don't think that will work, hold on a minute and I will ask."

Justin put his hand over the phone to ask if Andrew could stay with them. Elin looked over at Daniel, then shook her head. Daniel said that he would pay for a hotel room for Andrew, so Justin told Andrew the plan.

"Wow, thanks. Which hotel?"

"The one just down from the hostel would be the best, as it's close to food and everything else."

"That's cool. Thanks, bro."

Justin tensed up as he hung up the phone. Daniel dialled the hotel to pay for the room with his credit card. That would settle that for a little while. Daniel prayed that Heather called them back soon. He called his wife to let her know that he would be staying in town for a couple more days. She knew he wasn't telling her everything, but she trusted him enough to know he would tell her when the time was right. Justin asked if it was all right to go and have a shower. Elin nodded.

"Elin, we have one more thing to do, right?"

She nodded as Daniel picked up his phone to call Jason. Daniel gave him the whole story, then told him to make sure they were all taking precautions. Jason wanted to kick himself for getting involved with Andrew, but just possibly it would all work out as they walked through this. When he hung up, he told his grandparents what was going on. They just nodded their heads, hoping they weren't walking into something they couldn't manage.

Emma heard the phone ring, so she got on the stair lift to come down the stairs. They weren't sure what to tell her. They decided to just let it go for now. Iris got up to get Emma a cup of coffee and a slice of cake. The rest of them watched Iris. When she turned around to all the eyes looking at her, she decided it would be best to get all of them a piece of cake. Emma grinned a little as she watched them. Ziggy came prowling into the kitchen and found Jason's lap. It had been a long time since they had sat together in this kitchen. Scout barked outside, so Austin went out to the kennel to bring him inside. As soon as he got inside, he made a straight line to Emma. She hugged him as he unceremoniously flopped at her feet. No one could get by him, but he wasn't moving, at least not for now.

Jason looked out at the full moon and wondered what was going on in this crazy world. Who would want to hurt Emma? She had her fill of struggles, then there was today. Daniel thought it may have been Andrew that hit her but what could his reason be? Andrew seemed like a nice kid, so he wasn't going to start blaming him until everything was out in the open. He prayed that Heather would call Daniel soon. If they were able to help Andrew find his father, then the horizon would clear again, and they could start trying to find whoever hit Emma. The police wanted to talk with them tomorrow. They had examined the garden while the family was away at the hospital, but they didn't find much, even with the canine unit.

Emma and the grandparents went to sit in the living room to watch a little TV. The night was incredibly beautiful as the moon shone in through the living room window. Scout sat at Emma's chair as the grandparents took turns petting Ziggy. When the late news came on, the phone rang, Jason went to answer it. He took the call in the kitchen. When he came out of the kitchen the grandparents knew it had been Daniel calling back. He didn't say anything but just went upstairs.

Heather took a moment to pull her thoughts together. It had been more difficult than she had imagined talking with Roy about Andrew. When she started asking him about Andrew, she could see the wall go up. Because of the sensitivity of the subject, she just took a soft approach. Roy sat back down on his chair as he looked over at Heather with tears in his eyes. Yes, he had been involved with some of the things that had affected Heather and her kidnapping.

Now he felt he owed her on this one. He took a deep breath as he started his response.

"Heather, my life has not always been one where I looked out for more than myself. It wasn't until I lost you that I realised how lonely life could be. For many of the people I met, and used along the way, I feel deep shame. I knew Andrew's mother but up until now I didn't realise that there was a child involved. He could be my son but I'm not 100% sure of that."

Heather took the words in and was beginning to formulate the next step. There would need to be a paternity test. She wondered if they would both agree to it, but she felt there was no other option at this point.

"Would you be willing to undergo a paternity test?" Heather asked.

"As long as my privacy is upheld, I would take the test. You know that I need to stay out of the spotlight, especially with something like this."

"Would you be OK with me talking to Daniel about this? He is in the best spot to be the intermediary. Also, if he is controlling the information then you know he'd keep you safe as well."

"That's fine. I need to go now. Talk to you in the morning."

"Good night, Roy. See you tomorrow."

Heather picked up the phone and called Daniel back. The call was short but to the point. Daniel seemed to be willing to manage things that would need to be setup like the paternity test and any follow-ups. Heather asked to speak to Elin. She asked Elin to help them keep this quiet. At first, Elin was a little unsure about that, but once Heather explained the circumstances, she agreed to their plan. Daniel went upstairs to call Jason with the information he was able to share.

Jason was sitting in his room staring out the window when Austin went upstairs to go to the washroom. There was no doubt the moon took a magnificent picture in the pitch-black sky. Austin knocked on Jason's door. Jason turned towards him with tears in his eyes.

"What's up, Jason?"

"It's this whole thing with Emma. Are we about to go through another round of incidents and fear?"

"What did Daniel have to say, was it something that made you concerned about our safety?"

"Not really. Roy is willing to do the paternity test as long as his whereabouts is kept quiet."

"Is it that Emma was attacked?"

"Exactly. She has gone through so much. Who would want to hurt her?"

"The party guests all get a pass, including Justin. So, who, outside of that group, would want to trespass?"

"Right. That's the question."

Austin gave Jason a hug. They both went downstairs to join Iris and Emma in the living room. Jason was missing his parents big time but that was because of Emma and her push to recover, then this incident. Physically, mentally, and emotionally she had made the journey into wellness. For that reason, Jason and Austin had agreed that for tonight, they were unwilling to say too much. However, they knew that sooner rather than later, she would be asking questions. They had decided that once she started to ask questions, they would answer her truthfully. Scout perked up his ears as they came into the room. Emma was staring at the TV not wanting to think about what had happened as Junior and grandpa came back to sit with them.

"So, I can see that something is happening. So far, we haven't talked about what happened earlier. Is there something I should know?" Emma asked.

"Well," grandpa said. "What would you like to know?"

"First, who hit me and why?"

"Those are good questions; we don't have a definitive answer just yet. There are a couple of possibilities."

"Oh, yah, most of the people I know were at the party. I was the only one of them to go outside."

"So, we can conclude that it wasn't one of your friends or family."

"OK. Who do you think would do this?" Emma asked.

"We're not sure, Emma," Jason said. "However, we are thinking of people who have just recently put themselves in our lives, like Andrew."

"That's an interesting thought. What is he looking for anyway?"

"He's looking for his father," Austin answered.

"Oh. Well, how would that involve me?"

"That's the big question. We just don't know."

"It's all good. I love being home here with Scout and Ziggy, and all of you. The rest we will just deal with."

Her grandma looked over at her, wondering if she knew that she sounded like her father. It made them all stop and look at her. She looked back at them wondering why they were all staring at her. Emma told them she wanted to shower, then have her bedtime tea. Iris smiled, promising that she would have it set out by the time she came back downstairs.

Jason and Austin watched as Emma got on the stair lift to go upstairs to the bathroom. They shook their heads, wondering where she got all her strength. Jason and Austin went upstairs to check the outside camera. The security system's computer was in his father's old office. They brought up the file to watch the cameras on both backyard entry points. They saw a figure open the side gate, then head towards the shed as the back door opened. As much as they tried to clarify the picture, it did not give them enough to distinguish who it was. They made a copy of the file to give to the police in the morning.

They heard the bathroom door open as Emma made her way to her bedroom to dress for bed. Scout was waiting outside the bathroom door, so he followed her to her room. She wondered how her other grandparents were doing. She gave them a quick call to wish them both a good night. After drying her hair, Emma got dressed for bed. Ziggy came up to her door and scratched on the outside, so she let him in. Emma took a good look at her braces. She was thankful they hadn't been damaged. In fact, they may have saved her from greater injury. There was an appointment with the surgeon, later next week. Other than a little pain in her right leg, everything seemed fine. Emma knew it would be so great to be finished with the surgeries. Just two more, then done!

Emma headed downstairs for her tea. It was her way of remembering her mom and dad who religiously followed their tea routine every night. Grandma Iris had made her favourite biscuits for her party, so she knew they would make it to the table tonight. When she got to the kitchen, she found Junior and the grandparents waiting for her. Iris poured the tea, as they all reached into the biscuit pile for their favourite.

These were the best times. Emma smiled as she watched them all. Grandma noticed a little cut on her leg, so Emma looked down at it. It wasn't bleeding or anything. It could have been made by the braces. They finished off their tea and biscuits then Iris and Austin went to watch TV, as Jason and Emma headed to bed.

Chapter Six

Andrew woke up wondering where he was for a moment. Then he remembered that he was back in Allerton. He thought about what the day would bring. Knowing that Jason would make contact later today, gave him mixed feelings. He had heard that Jason's sister had been hurt, he also knew that his appearance in Allerton could make him a suspect. They really didn't know him at all. Justin did, but they were bound by the secrets they shared. Jason knew he was looking for his father, but he didn't know there were two possibilities. Andrew's phone rang, it was his mother, so he picked up his phone.

"Hi, Mom."

"Andrew, where are you? I thought you were upstairs but when I went up to look for you, you were gone."

"I'm back in Allerton. I need to find out about my father."

"Andrew, please don't do this. It will bring up a lot of old baggage."

"I know, and I'm sorry. But some of that baggage is mine. I need to know."

The hotel phone rang. Andrew told his mother he had to go. It was Jason inviting him downstairs for breakfast with him and Daniel. Andrew headed downstairs wondering what Daniel was like. He took a deep breath as he stepped into the restaurant. Jason waved him over to the table as Andrew watched Daniel watch him.

"Daniel, I would like to introduce Andrew. Andrew, this is Daniel. He's Elin and Heather's brother."

Andrew sat down, watching Daniel and Jason. Maybe this could work out yet.

"Hi, Daniel. Good to see you, Jason," Andrew said as he picked up the menu.

"Breakfast is on me," Daniel stated. "Have whatever you want."

"Thanks. I'll just have the breakfast special."

They all ordered the special and the coffee started to flow. Andrew wasn't sure what was going to happen, but he hoped for some answers. After breakfast arrived, Daniel looked over at Andrew.

"Andrew, I hear that you think my sister's ex may be your father. What gives you that idea?"

"Well…my mom told me several years ago that she believed that Roy Ahns was my father. I looked around for him but there was literally no trace of him to be found. He has no surviving family other that your sister, so that was where I started."

"That is an interesting possibility. I have been in touch with my sister who in turn spoke with her ex about your claim. He is willing to take a paternity test if you are so inclined."

"What! You know where he is?"

"Not really, but my sister does. He still requests his privacy, and you would have to respect that."

"So, he doesn't want to see me?"

"I didn't say that. It would be prudent to do the paternity test first, then we could move on from there."

"OK, I guess that would at least be a start. I do have to be honest with you though. He may not be my father, there is another possibility."

"Yes, Justin filled us in on the other possibility. Still, it would be good to get this test done. It would be best for you, and for Roy, at this point. He claims that he was never informed that he had a child."

"That is what I was told as well."

They ate their breakfast in relative silence until they were all finished. Next thing to do was to get the testing done. Daniel called Elin to see if she would ask her doctor about the procedure for getting a paternity test in town. She was glad to be able to help.

Her doctor told her he could issue a lab form for the procedure, he would just need to know Andrew's full name and health care number. He also mentioned that Roy Ahns would need to take a similar test and have the results sent to him. He noted that Andrew could go to his own doctor to request the same procedure. Daniel, Andrew, and Jason discussed the possibilities. The three of them decided having it done in town would be best. Besides, Daniel was willing to foot any of the costs.

Daniel called Elin back to tell her their decision. She called her doctor with Andrew's information so he could send the form on through to the lab. Elin then called Heather to let her know that Roy would need to do the same test and have the results sent to her doctor in Allerton. As they were all together, Jason offered to drive Andrew to the clinic to have the test. While they waited at the clinic, Jason stopped in at the pharmacy to pick up a prescription for Emma. She showed no outward signs of injury, but it was still causing her a fair amount of pain.

Emma looked down when she felt a twinge in her leg, but she just put it down to yesterday's fall. The grandparents looked up as she came into the kitchen for breakfast. It was good to have her there with them. The other grandparents were going to take a quick trip to the mainland to check up on their house. They had told Emma they would be back in about a week, but she could phone them every day if she wanted.

Emma would miss having both sets of grandparents there. She decided to finish her breakfast then go upstairs to work on her computer. She was looking at design schools in the area, especially online ones or ones that had their school on the island. After an hour of searching, Emma got up to go into her mom's studio. She had put the painting she was working on for Junior in there, as she didn't think he would go into that room. She got her painting supplies ready and started on her copy of the, Unfinished Life, painting. This time she was using mixed colours that flowed across the colour spectrum. She would never be a painter, but this one needed to be perfect.

Just as she finished the main colour of paint, her phone rang in her bedroom. She walked back to her room and saw it was Justin.

"Hello."

"Hi, Emma. Just wondering how you're doing?"

"I'm doing pretty good. Working on the painting I want to give Junior when he completes his engineering programme."

"Wow, that is impressive. I didn't know that you painted."

"I don't, usually. This is just a special project."

"Do you want to go out for a walk along the river this afternoon?"

"I'd love to, but I have been having a little difficulty with my right leg."

"Well, then, we'll walk as far as you feel you are able."

"Sounds good. It looks beautiful outside."

"It is. Meet you at the marina?"

"Okay, I'll see if my grandparents can drop me down there."

"If they can't, let me know."

"Will do. Bye, Justin."

Emma went into the washroom to wash her hands and brushes. The sink in the studio was full of other things. She took the stair lift downstairs to ask her grandma if they could drop her off at the marina so she and Justin could go for a walk. That was no problem as they were heading into town anyway. Emma stair-lifted back upstairs, got her braces and walking shoes on, then grabbed a jacket just in case. By the time she was downstairs, both grandparents were waiting for her in the living room. Life would have been so much more difficult without both sets of her grandparents sticking around to help them through all of this. She gave them each a hug. They just looked at one another and smiled.

Andrew went through the steps needed for his paternity test, then went out to the waiting area expecting Jason and Daniel to have left. They were still sitting there waiting for him. Daniel told him that he could drive him home, so he accepted his offer, but he had to pick up his things at the hotel. They were all kind of quiet as they hit the motorway, so Daniel asked Andrew a few questions. Then he asked Andrew if he could take a picture to send to his sister who in turn would be able to show it to Roy. Andrew didn't have any problem with that. Daniel asked him if he would tell his mother about the paternity test. Andrew told them that was the plan, but he would need to find the right way to do so. They nodded their heads in agreement. When they reached Andrew's house, his mother came out of the house.

"Andrew, good to see you. Thank you for bringing him home."

"No problem. We had a good chat, so time went by quite quickly. We only know you as Andrew's mom. I'm not sure you want us to call you that."

"I'm Marley. Marley Sullivan. Daniel, I knew your mom and dad way back then."

"Ms. Sullivan, my folks had a wide circle of friends. I'm glad you were one of them."

"Well, thanks, guys. Will give you a call the next time I get to Allerton," Andrew said with a grin.

"For sure, Andrew. Take care."

On the way home, Jason and Daniel chatted a little about Andrew as well as about the paternity issue. They also talked about Emma's fall. Jason made sure to let Daniel know that Emma was doing well. He said the grandparents had messaged him to tell him they were taking her to the marina to go for a walk with Justin.

When they stopped at the petrol station to fill up, Daniel went into the coffee shop to pick them up coffee. Jason mentioned he had met Andrew at this station. Andrew certainly liked to wander. It looked like it was difficult for his mother to keep track of him. He was at least 16 years old. However, he behaved like he was much older. According to their calculations, he may have one more year in school before post-secondary.

Daniel asked Jason what his plans were for when he finished his programme, but Jason shrugged his shoulders. Then Jason started telling Daniel about wanting to locate on the island, maybe even in Allerton. So much of today's business was done online that physical location wasn't a big deal anymore. That was unless you were in the big league with offices in the major city centres. They talked a little about Rosa, then Daniel teased Jason a little. Jason told Daniel that he was serious about her but didn't know how well she would fit into a small town. He told Daniel that she grew up in a bigger city and she often made trips to the mainland just for shopping. Daniel smiled at Jason. He told him he just needed to let things work themselves out, that he shouldn't make any rash decisions based on unsound data. Jason looked over at Daniel and smiled, what else could you expect from an accountant, no matter how wise he was.

Daniel dropped Jason off at the restaurant, then headed back to Elin's house. Her doctor had told her that it could be up to a week before the paternity results came back. Daniel figured he would stay on until the paternity tests were complete. When he talked to Elin and Justin, they seemed ok with his extended stay. It would also give him a chance to see if Justin wanted to come onside with his accounting firm. They were looking for student interns this summer, and summer would be the perfect testing ground for something more.

Elin had coffee made when Daniel got home. Daniel thought it could be a good time to talk with Justin about the summer. Elin picked up Fancy to cuddle her. They talked a little about Andrew, but Justin just shut down when the topic came up. Daniel thought he would broach the subject of summer internship as that could be beneficial for both Justin and Daniel.

"Justin, have you found any job for the summer?"

"No, not really. School has just finished. Some of the tourist businesses are just starting to hire."

"Would you be interested in interning at my firm this summer? Each summer, we take on a couple of student interns to manage holiday time for our full-time employees."

Justin looked over at Elin. She just smiled back at him. He was going to help Elin on her boat, but this intern thing seemed like a promising idea. He would be away from Emma, but she had a couple of surgeries to do as well as setting up her studies for the autumn. They could still chat, and text. It wasn't that far from Allerton to the southern tip of the island.

"That would be cool. I would like to give it a try."

"It would be challenging work. You would be expected to work full-time hours. I know you have the stuff that it takes. I can get your paperwork started while I am here, maybe you could come with me when I head home in a few days?"

"Sure! I have my brother's car still, but I only have my beginners' licence. I haven't ever driven in the bigger cities."

"No worry. You could stay with us. There is a good transit system close by as well as being able to drive around with me and my wife. One of our daughters has her licence as well."

"Sounds like a plan. Thank you so much."

Justin headed to his room to text Emma. He hoped that she would be all right with this.

Daniel looked over at Elin to see her reaction, but she seemed lost in thought. He knew that it had been busy for some time, so they just sat quietly. There was a loud noise outside, then someone talking. Daniel glanced over at Elin before he remembered that it must be the midweek tsunami warning test the city did every other week. Even though they were above the inundation zone, it was good to know how to respond to the warning. It was close to 60 years since a tsunami caused any concern in this neck of the woods. However, it was important not to forget how much of a deadly force they could carry. Fancy got down off Elin's shoulder, so Elin let her outside for her exercise time. Daniel headed up to his room to find the paperwork that Justin would need to fill out. Hopefully, he could take a little nap before dinner.

Daniel woke up to a big boom sound and looked out his bedroom window. The sunshine had bumped into black storm clouds. There was another flash of lightning. Daniel counted by ones, to see how far away the lightning strike was. He counted up to twelve before he heard the thunder so if the stories were true, the strike was twelve miles away. He heard Elin letting Fancy in. Daniel heard her run into the house, stopping at Daniel's open bedroom door. The poor girl was soaked to her skin by the downpour that followed the thunder. He grabbed his housecoat to dry her off. She tried to jump onto his bed, so he lay the housecoat down and picked her up. There was another lightning flash, then more thunder. Fancy started to whimper, so Daniel picked her up in the housecoat to head down the hallway to find Elin. Justin was just coming out of his room, so they headed to the kitchen together. Elin was busy cooking up pasta and meatballs for dinner. She smiled as they came into the kitchen.

"Justin, I downloaded the paperwork you will need to fill out. I just need to print it out," Daniel mentioned.

"Email them to me and I can do that. I have a printer in my room for doing assignments."

"As soon as I can turn Fancy over to her owner, I will do just that."

Elin took Fancy from Daniel, so Daniel headed back down the hallway. Within a few minutes he was back in the kitchen.

"I sent you the paperwork, Justin. Once you have filled it out, we can scan it. I will email it to HR."

"I'll do that tonight. I told Emma about collaborating with you this summer and she seems happy about that. I told her we could still stay in touch. She mentioned that maybe Jason could drive her down the island for a visit. Do you think that would work?"

"Most definitely. Elin, what will you do with just you and Fancy here?"

"Well, I'm not sure but fishing season will be on and off all summer. Then I would like to head East to visit some of mom and dad's family. I'd take Fancy with me."

"What about Casey?"

"Casey is doing his own thing. We are friends but that's about all."

"Sorry to hear that. I know someone at work that is in a similar situation. Can I hook you two up?"

"NO! Let's just let things go forwards as they go forward."

Daniel giggled which sent the three of them into a laughing session.

The rain poured down as they watched the wind start to pick up. Elin got up to find the candles and lighter, just in case the power went out. Fancy hid under the table so Elin put the housecoat down so she could lay on it. Elin put dinner together then pulled the garlic bread out of the oven. Justin got up to set the table as Daniel put on the coffee maker. He asked Elin about dessert but she hadn't planned on anything so it would be biscuits and coffee for dessert. It all worked.

They were just finishing dinner when there was a big 'pop' sound as the lights flickered on and off. They grabbed their coffees, taking them into the living room so they could watch the storm better. Just as they got seated, the lights went out. Elin moved slowly into the kitchen to get the candles and lighter. Fancy followed her into the kitchen then back to the living room. They set the candles out as Daniel lit them. Then they sat down to watch nature's show.

A car pulled into the driveway. Elin and Daniel got up to see who it was. It was still light outside, so they recognised Heather's car. Elin opened the door and gave her a big hug.

"Are you here by yourself, or did Roy come with you?"

"Just me, at this point. I thought it would be good to be here as the circumstances play themselves out. It's so good to see you both, and you too, Justin," Heather said as she ducked inside.

Lightning lit up the sky as Fancy ran to hide under the coffee table. Elin picked her up and cuddled her as she sat back down on the sofa. Daniel saw that Heather had a suitcase, so he grabbed a candle to take the suitcase to her old room.

"Thanks, Daniel," Heather said as they reached the bedroom. "I haven't had dinner yet, is there something I can rustle up here?"

"I think there is some spaghetti left from our dinner."

"Just drop the suitcase there," Heather said. "I'll take care of it later."

"OK. I'll head to the kitchen to get your dinner. It should still be warm. You'll probably have to eat in the living room as the candles are all in there."

"Sounds good. I'm right behind you."

Justin sat in the living room and watched as the others got Heather her dinner. Once they got her settled in the living room, he thought he would sneak upstairs to give Emma a call. As he stepped into his room, he looked out the window. He could see the clouds forming against the sun. It truly was an amazing show. He picked up his phone to dial Emma.

"Hi, Justin," she answered.

"Hi, how's things at your place?"

"Good for now, and you?"

"Good. The lights just went out. Daniel and Heather are here so I thought I would give them some time to talk without me."

"Gram just bought in some coffee and biscuits. Do you want to join us?"

"Not tonight, maybe tomorrow. I just wanted to check in with you. I better go see what's happening here. See you tomorrow."

"Bye for now, Justin."

Emma put down her phone as their lights flickered, then went off. Austin got up, heading into the living room to find the candles while Iris fished for the lighter in one of the drawers. Scout sat at Emma's feet watching over her. Emma reached down to give him a hug, so he settled down again.

Not to be outdone, Ziggy scurried into the kitchen and planted himself on Jason's lap. His claws hung onto Jason's leg, so Jason gently picked up the paws as he gave Ziggy a pet. They had finished dinner a while back, so Iris got out the cinnamon buns and poured the remaining warm coffee into their mugs. Austin did a tour of the house to make sure that the windows were all shut. He was feeling a little uneasy but from the looks of things it was just a typical early summer storm.

The phone rang. Iris got up to answer it. It was the other set of grandparents checking up on all of them. They had just got home before the storm started. It was only rainy and windy so far. The kids both talked with them, then Iris chatted with them for a while. They had become quite a cohesive group over the last few years, for that Iris was thankful. Both sets of grandparents did not want the grandkids to feel abandoned. They had worked out a good system.

Austin put batteries in his radio then turned it on to see if there was any news. He found a station from the mainland where he could listen to the news. When it went back to music, Austin turned the volume down but still left it on.

Rosa sent a text to Jason to see how they were doing, so he told her all was well. He asked how she was. She sent him a big smiley face so he figured that she must be working on her designs. He missed her a lot even though they hadn't been apart that long. Jason remembered that he was going to work on his assignments, but he would leave it for tonight, he felt exhausted. As he finished his conversation with Rosa, he decided to go to his room to lie down. Within minutes, he was asleep.

Emma went to her room, ready for bed as well. She took a candle into her room and pulled out her drawing pad. She decided that she wanted to design a set of clothes based on the thunder and lightning, they would be both bold and dark. By the time she looked up, she heard the grandparents heading to bed. Scout jumped up on her bed as Ziggy crawled up on it. Looking over her designs, she felt if she could pull it all together it would fit well in her portfolio. She put down her drawing pad then headed to the washroom to get ready for bed. Her braces were still sitting in the washroom, so she picked them up to take them into her room for the night.

Just as Emma pulled the blankets up, there was a knock on the front door. She waited to see if the grandparents got up, but she didn't think they heard it. Pulling back the blankets, she put on her slippers and went downstairs on the stair lift. Feeling a little anxious, she looked out the window but couldn't see anyone on the porch. There was another knock on the door, so Emma went to the door to open it. Before she could get it open, Jason was at her side. She let her breath out. He opened the door to find Melanie Hayes from next door.

Chapter Seven

Jason and Emma moved away from the door to let Melanie in. It had been quite a while since any of them had seen her. After her dad passed away, Melanie got quiet and a little introverted. The three of them had gone to school around the same time, and Jason had always considered her a friend.

Melanie was shivering so Emma grabbed a blanket off the chair to wrap around her, wondering why Melanie was out at this time of night. They heard someone go into the washroom upstairs. A few minutes later Iris came downstairs in her housecoat. The power was still out so Iris lit the candles in the living room then tossed some wood into the fireplace. Even though the fan was electrically powered, they also had a battery back up for it, so soon the flames flickered up and started to warm the living room.

Austin got up as well. He went to the utility room to find his battery-operated electronics charger which could take several plug-ins. The grandkids had all gone together to get him one, after the last difficult winter. Iris plugged in the coffeemaker as well as a kettle to make hot chocolate. The wind was still howling, so Scout found his place near Emma and snuggled down. Ziggy was full of energy. He went from one person to another to get a pet.

"What brings you out on a night like this, Melanie?" Austin asked.

"I went out with Raymond, but when we got home the door was locked. He couldn't find his key."

"Where is Raymond now?" Jason asked.

"In his pickup truck. He didn't want to disturb anyone, but I was freezing so I took a chance that someone here would be awake."

Jason went upstairs to get his phone so that he could message Raymond to join them. There was no answer back but a few minutes later they heard someone on the outside steps. Iris opened the door to let Raymond in. He was shivering so she took his jacket as she grabbed him a blanket from the closet. He sat on the sofa next to Melanie. Iris brought him a cup of coffee.

"Melanie was saying you couldn't get into the house. Did you lose your keys?" Jason asked.

"No, I think I left them in my room. Mom is a deep sleeper, especially if she takes her medication," Raymond explained.

"Thank you for taking us in. I know it's a little late for a visit but we were out of options at this point," Melanie added.

They chatted for a while, then Iris found blankets and a pillow so Raymond could sleep on the sofa. Emma took Melanie upstairs to the guest room. Once they were all settled, Austin snuffed out the fireplace and headed back to bed. Just as Emma pulled her blankets up, the lights came back on. She got up to turn off her bedroom light. Looking downstairs, she saw that all the lights were off. She cuddled back into her blankets as she fell asleep.

When Emma awoke, she heard voices downstairs. She looked over at her alarm clock that was flashing on and off, so she got up. Looking through her closet, she found something for Melanie to change into. With a casual suit in her hands, Emma headed to Melanie's bedroom. The door was already open, and Melanie wasn't there, so she hung the items in the room then headed downstairs. As she neared the kitchen, she could hear Jason and Raymond talking, but when she came into the kitchen they stopped. She wondered what was going on but decided that it wasn't that important. Grabbing a cup of coffee, she sat at the table.

"Melanie, I left an outfit for you in the bedroom. You are welcome to wear it. In fact, just keep it. It's one I designed last semester."

"Oh! Thanks! I can bring it back if you want."

"No, just keep it, I have a lot of clothing, don't I, Junior?"

"You wouldn't believe the amount of clothing she has. I guess it's part of the trade she's involved in."

Emma smiled as she gave him a little punch in the arm. It really was nice to be together, even if it was only for a short while. Melanie headed upstairs to change while Raymond put his blankets and pillow in a pile on the recliner. When Melanie came downstairs, she looked amazing in the outfit Emma had left her. She gave Emma a hug. Both her and Raymond thanked the Ryan's for taking them in.

"So, what were you and Raymond discussing before I came into the kitchen?"

Emma asked after Raymond had left.

"Just stuff. Nothing to worry about."

"OK, for now. I think I may have found the design school that I want to attend. It's online, only the final fashion shows each semester will be in one of the larger cities on the island or on the mainland."

"Are you sure that is what you want? I know there is a good-sized educational account that you can draw on." Jason replied.

"I think I found the one I want but I can look around a wee bit more. What about you, what will you do once you're done with school?"

"Good question. I want to stay on the island. My training will allow me to work wherever I want but I will also need to be connected online with some sort of firm."

"How serious are you and Rosa?" Emma asked.

"That's the one thing that may change my decision. I'm not sure she would want to stay on the island, she is used to bigger cities."

"You've got a couple of months to think about it but don't leave it too long. Let her know what you're thinking, you may be surprised."

"Have you talked about it?"

"Not fully. I know she has feelings for you. She seems to like the family and friends she has met so far."

"Good to know, thanks."

"I do have a favour to ask of you though."

"What would that be?"

"Justin is going to work with Daniel at his firm. Could you take me down to visit a time or two this summer?"

"We could work something out. Now it's my turn, how serious are you and Justin?"

"I really don't know. We are more than just good friends but it's hard to get any closer with our family histories."

"It's good to take it slow, Emma. You have lots of time. After your surgeries are done, you can plan away."

"That was my thought, too. I don't think the bat in the knees did any real damage. They don't hurt too much or cause me pain when I walk."

"Excellent. It would still be good to know who did that."

"It would for sure."

There was a knock at the front door, so Jason went to answer it. He came back with the other set of grandparents. They were carrying the portrait of their dad all framed. Emma and Jason just stood there staring at the portrait. Iris and Austin wandered in to see who was there. When they saw the painting, they gasped. Austin rubbed his eyes as Iris tried not to cry. They talked about where it should hang before deciding it would be best in the upper hallway. He would always be in the middle of the family. Jason took it upstairs and held it in place while the grandparents rethought its positioning.

After the picture was hung, they decided to all go out for lunch, so they filled a couple of vehicles and headed into town. They chose to go to Food World, partly because Jason had worked there, partly because they had a wide variety of food on their menu. Jason got up from their table and went to chat with Aaron, who was still managing the restaurant. Emma saw Justin sitting with Elin's family and his mother. She contemplated going over to see them but there was a little fear left, she didn't know what his mother thought of her.

Feeling tired of running away, Emma headed over to their table to greet them all. She told Justin that Jason was willing to take her to visit a couple times during the summer. Emma caught the swift movement his mother made. Elin told Emma she could help her go visit as well. She thanked her then headed back to her table. She wasn't just imagining it; his mother still didn't like them seeing each other. However, if she looked at her own family, she could say the same for several of them. Time would tell.

After lunch they all wanted to go for a walk along the river as the sun was radiating down from a very blue sky. They walked up to the telescope, then headed back to their vehicles. Jason was going home to work on some of his assignments. Emma was hoping to do a little more searching for design schools.

Alison's parents told them they were heading to the mainland today to check up on their house. It had been several months since they had been home, and it felt like the right time to go. Emma gave them each a hug, trying not to look at them as she still felt a little scared that they were leaving. Iris grabbed Emma's hand. The warmth gave her the strength to smile at her mom's parents as they divided up into vehicles again.

When they got home, there was a message on the answering machine telling Emma that her first surgery was booked for the 15th at the regional hospital in the town where Jason went to school. They mustn't have found any damage after her fall. She felt like this was truly the end of an extensive line of surgeries. She couldn't wait until she could walk anywhere without the braces, but she knew they had made it possible to achieve what she had achieved. There was also a message from Raymond for Jason to give him a call, which was a little odd as they just saw each other this morning. Again, Emma wondered what was going on with the two of them. She wrote down the message to give to Jason.

Emma went up to her room and started her Internet search until Justin started sending her messages. Apparently, he would be leaving at the end of next week. He was looking forward to a fresh start somewhere else. That concerned Emma a little, but she knew the kind of pressure he had been living under. It was a tough ride between him and his mother. Yet he still loved her wholeheartedly. However, he believed it was best for both of them if he continued to stay with Elin. Elin was willing to work with that. Elin and her siblings had actually made Justin a part of their family. Emma understood as she had the same amazing bond with her family. She decided to go down to the kitchen for a soda. As she got to the kitchen door the conversation her grandparents and Jason were having ended. That was odd but she had other things to think about today.

"Hey, Emma. Can I let Rosa know about your upcoming surgery? She would love to visit you while you're in the hospital."

"Sure, you can tell her. I meant to do that but between looking for a school and sending out text messages to Justin, it slipped my mind."

"Is everything OK with Justin? I noticed you didn't stay long at their table."

"It was OK. I don't think his mother likes us being friends but it's not going to stop us."

"Good thinking," her grandma said as she gave her a hug.

"Thanks, Gram."

Jason picked up some papers off the table as he headed back upstairs. Emma got the feeling like something had gone on, but she wasn't able to put it all together, yet. She grabbed a soda and a couple of biscuits then headed back upstairs on the stair lift. Sometimes, she used it just because it was part of her recovery. Sometimes it made her smile as she remembered her dad using it to get upstairs when they were both newly out of the hospital. She looked up at his portrait as she headed to her room.

Getting back to her search for schools, she didn't notice that Jason headed back downstairs. After going through a dozen schools, Emma decided to take a short nap as the night before had been a little messed up. She snuggled into her bed and then heard someone let Scout in. She heard him heading down the hallway. He looked in the room, so she called him up on the bed. The two of them closed their eyes and napped.

There was a light knock on the bedroom door. Scout's ears perked up as he jumped off the bed, which was enough to awake Emma. She turned towards the door. It was her grandma. Emma waved her in.

"Dinner is almost ready, Emma. It's probably time to get up, you have about 15 minutes."

"Thanks, Gram. What time is it?"

"It's quarter to six."

"Wow, I have been sleeping for a while. I guess we all lost a little sleep last night. How are you and grandpa doing?"

"Grandpa had a bit of a nap. I sat in the recliner but dozed off for a bit. We all had a little sleep so we're all ready for whatever comes next."

Emma smiled as she pulled off the blankets. The smell of roast chicken wafted up the hallway as Emma headed to the washroom. She could hear Jason and the grandparents downstairs and knew they were waiting for her, so she quickly got on the stair lift. Scout walked with her to the bottom of the stairs. It was good being home with him again. Ziggy started to rub against Scout, Emma had to smile at Scout's expression, he was so tolerant. When Emma landed at the bottom, she gave Scout a hug, picked up Ziggy, and took him into the kitchen with her. The family was all seated at the table, so Emma gave Ziggy to Jason as she sat down.

"I think I've found the school I want to attend, it's based on the island and has a fully online curriculum except, of course, for the fashion shows."

"That sounds great!" Jason said with a smile.

"Junior, I've been working on something special for when you graduate. When is that exactly?"

"It is supposed to be at the end of December, but I'll have finished all the modules by the end of September. At least that is what it looks like."

"Wow, so what happens after that?"

"Not sure yet. I have a few things to figure out."

"You, two, enough work talk, let's eat our dinner," their grandpa said with a smile.

After dinner, Emma and Jason shooed the grandparents into the living room while they did the dishes. For some reason, it just all felt so right. They put on the coffee, cut the pie, and took it to the grandparents. Emma grabbed some cups with coffee fixings and put them on a tray. She waited while the coffee finished brewing, then took it all into the living room. Just as they all got comfortable, the phone rang, so Austin got up to answer it.

"Hello."

"Mr. Ryan, this is Constable Allen from the Allerton police. We have had a development in the case concerning your granddaughter."

"Oh, is it good or bad?"

"Not sure how to classify this, I guess it depends on who is listening. Adrianne Knowles just popped into the office to tell us that she had been out hunting and had hit something."

"OK. How is that relevant?"

"It appears that she is off her medications. We think she may have struck Emma while she was not present in this world."

"How did she get away so quickly?"

"Good question. I don't have an answer for that at this time."

"OK. Thanks for the update. Where is Adrianne now?"

"We talked to her remaining family. They decided she would be more likely to recover at the Mental Health Recovery Centre."

"That sounds logical. I'll pass along what you have told me."

“We haven’t closed the case completely, but this seems like a possible explanation.”

“Thanks for your work, officer.”

“Good night, Mr. Ryan. Give our best to the family.”

Austin put the phone down and thought about the best way to approach this for the good of the family. He sat down then told the family what the officer had told him. They saw Emma cringe as she looked at her phone. They sat quiet for a moment or so, then Emma looked up.

“I am doing well physically, there was no long-term damage. I know Justin’s mom has her issues and I’m not willing to put her behaviour on him. I still like him, as a friend or maybe even more than that. We’ll see what happens from here.”

“Good thinking, kiddo,” Jason said. “When did you grow up so much?”

“I was taking up the slack that you left behind,” Emma said as she smiled at Jason.

Jason went over to give her a gentle shove as Scout watched. Jason picked up his phone and called Elin who wanted to be kept up to date on how Emma was doing. She probably already knew about Adrianne, but it would be good to chat it through. He dialled the phone and let it ring.

Elin’s phone rang. Justin looked over at Elin who was lost in thought. She looked at her phone, then turned it off. He wondered if she regretted taking him in with all the trouble in his family over the past few years. She noticed he was looking at her.

“Sorry, Justin. I was lost in thought for a moment. How are you doing with this newest set of events?”

“I don’t know. I’m glad that I’ll be leaving when Daniel goes but I will miss you. You have given me what I never had before, a place that is safe and a family that treats me like I was one of them.”

“You are one of us. Maybe not in name but in sharing our lives. I want you to always be able to come back here. Here being home.”

Justin looked away for a moment as he didn’t want to start crying. Other than his brother, Trevor, he had no one who took him under their wing like Elin had. He felt accepted by Daniel and Heather as well, even with what his parents had done. He was going to miss Emma this summer, but they had already made plans for her to visit him while he was working. Then there was his mother. No matter what she did, she was his mother. She was still unstable. So far, none of her treatments had been successful over a long period of time.

Elin’s phone rang again. She didn’t recognise the number, so she turned it off. What they had to figure out was enough for today. Andrew called Justin’s number, but it was busy. He just sat there on the balcony, looking at the river as he watched the moon shine upon the water. This was where he went to think things through but there were so many unanswered questions that sometimes he just wanted to give up, to move away. There was only one problem with that, it didn’t resolve any of the questions. It didn’t make things right or show any degree of reality. He leaned his head in his hands then decided to call it a day. He still needed to call his mom to let her know that he was okay before she checked to see if he was in his bedroom. He liked being here by the river as it gave him an inner sense of peace, but he knew that his mother worried, a lot.

"Hi, Mom."

"Hi, Andrew. Are you calling me from upstairs?"

"No, I'm in Allerton at the river. I just need to think. This seems like the best place to do it."

"Whereabouts in Allerton?"

"It's a place by the river. I know the people who live here. They have gone away for a few days. I'm sort of house-sitting."

"You should probably come home, Andrew. Do the people know that you are in their house?"

"It doesn't matter. I won't hurt anything. No one is here but me."

"Andrew, that is illegal. What if they come home unexpectedly?"

"Then I will clear out. I will see them coming before they get here. I am on the top balcony; it is so beautiful."

"Come home, Andrew. Please."

"I'll come home tomorrow, Mom. Don't worry. I am fine."

"Tomorrow, for sure?"

"For sure."

"OK. Get some sleep and keep in touch. Is there anything I can help you with?"

"Not tonight, Mom. Not tonight."

"Good night, Andrew."

"Good night."

Andrew ended the call, then went looking for a place to plug in his phone. He loved it up on the top level of the house. He had put some blankets and a pillow in the attic room that had its own balcony. He looked around a little until he found some of Emma's designs. It felt a little like he was going through her personal things, so he turned around and headed for the blankets and pillow. His phone said that it was almost 11 pm, it had been a long day. He wondered if Roy was his father or was Justin's father his father. Why did it matter so much, Justin's father was dead and Roy, he had no idea how Roy was. However, he saw that Heather Gray was in town. He realised that it probably had something to do with him. Would she like him? He wasn't like Justin, or her nieces and nephews. He tossed and turned a few times before he slept.

Andrew woke to a rumbling that was unlike anything he remembered hearing before. He looked out at the balcony and could see a little movement, but it was still unclear what was happening. It was daylight so maybe there was some heavy equipment being moved nearby, that would explain it. He lay back down. As he looked at the ceiling, his phone started to make weird sounds, so he grabbed it from the plug in. Flipping through the apps on his phone he saw one was blinking, something to do with earthquakes. He didn't remember putting the app on it so it must have come with the phone. He opened it up to see that there had been a small earthquake at the north end of the island. They had felt a little shaking even down here in Allerton. Andrew looked at the clock. Seeing it was just after 9 am, he put a call through to his mother.

"Hello, Andrew. I guess you felt the shaking down where you are too?"

"Sure did. It was the weirdest feeling, especially being on the top level of the house."

"Are you heading home now?"

"Not yet, Mom. I have a few things I want to do this morning, but I should be home by tonight."

"OK. I'll be watching for you. Will it be before dinner time?"

"Most likely. I'll let you know if my plans change."

"Take care, Andrew. I will wait dinner until you get here."

"OK, Mom. Bye."

"Bye, my dear."

Andrew looked out on the balcony. He took a few steps outside, testing to see if it was strong enough to hold him. After the shaking, he wanted to make sure it was safe. He sat out on the chair as he watched the clouds dissipate and the sun come through. Yes, it was going to be a beautiful day.

Chapter Eight

Emma wandered into the hallway, where she saw her dad's portrait swaying on the wall. Scout leaned against her whimpering, so Emma reached down to give him a pet. The door to Jason's room opened as he stepped out into the hallway. He peered at Emma and Scout, then noticed the portrait on the wall. It was time to get up anyway, but the rumbling was a little disconcerting. From downstairs, Emma and Jason heard the grandparents talking a little louder than normal. Emma grabbed the stair lift as she headed downstairs with Jason right behind her. When she got to the kitchen doorway, the grandparents were seated at the table holding hands.

"What's going on?" Jason asked.

"Well, it looks like the earth is shaking a little, so we think it's probably an earthquake."

"An earthquake? We had a bit of one a few days ago but this one is a little more active," Emma said. "What should we do?"

"Grab some coffee then come sit down. There are some cinnamon buns warming in the oven," Iris answered as she got up to get them from the oven.

Emma and Jason sat down as they looked out the kitchen window. Earthquakes were uncanny, it didn't seem to matter if it was sunny, or rainy, or anything. They just happened. Ziggy came into the kitchen. He jumped up on Jason's lap as he made his way to his shoulder. Jason held him close. Slowly Ziggy let go of his grip on Jason's shoulder. The rumbling quit, they all felt relieved except for one thing. They needed to check to make sure there was no tsunami following the shake. Jason pulled up his app. It told him that there was tsunami information being calculated. They were safe up there on Elk Drive but the people along the river, not so much.

Jason's phone rang so he answered it quickly.

"Hello, Jason. It's Rosa. I just wanted to make sure you were all safe."

"We're good for now, Rosa. Just waiting to see if there are any signs of a tsunami. How are you doing?"

"I'm good. Our dorms are high enough no tsunami would reach us, but the ground rolled and rumbled. Someone said it might be caused by liquefaction, but I haven't a clue what that is."

"From what I can remember, liquefaction is when the strength and stiffness of a soil is reduced by earthquake shaking. It's been responsible for a lot of damage during some earthquakes."

"Well, good thing I know an engineer. Should I be concerned about that?"

"They may evacuate the dorms until an inspection can make sure the foundation and retaining walls aren't damaged. If that happens, just drive on down here. We'll find you a place to stay."

"Thanks, Jason. I guess I should call my folks to let them know I'm OK. I'll give you a call a little later."

"OK, Rosa. Stay in touch."

"Will do."

Jason hung up his phone and looked around the table. All of them were looking at him so he blushed a little. He got up from the table to head upstairs to change. He heard them giggling as he left the kitchen. Ziggy followed him upstairs, pushing open his bedroom door so he could climb onto the bed. Jason sat with Ziggy for a few minutes, then decided to get dressed. There was a lot to get done. He was hoping that Andrew's paternity test results would come back today so he could go back to school. He had committed to being in Allerton until then. He wondered how Andrew and his mother were doing this morning.

Emma got up to answer the phone, then called grandpa. It was Alison's parents. They were wondering if he and Jason could go to the cottage to make sure everything was all right. Austin agreed to go over, he knew that Jason would have no problem going with him. The all-clear signal went off, telling everyone that there was no tsunami expected. That was an exceptionally good way to start the day.

Daniel and Elin heard the all-clear warning and also felt the relief. They looked around the house, wondering if next time they would have to head to higher ground. Their place wasn't that low down, but it was part of what was called the inundation zone. Justin came downstairs and looked over at the two of them. He poured himself a cup of coffee as Elin took some biscuits out of the oven.

Sitting around the table, they saw Fancy scuttle into the kitchen looking for breakfast. Elin picked her up to give her a hug. Then she put her down so she could get Fancy's breakfast. Daniel was on his phone talking with his wife. He was telling her that he and Justin would be heading their way in the next day or so. Justin looked up as he smiled at the opportunity to leave this town, to try something new. The only part he wasn't keen about was being that far from Emma. He hadn't told many people, not even Emma, how he felt about her. The tough dynamics between the two families as well as his concerns about how his mother may take it, made him careful about his feelings.

Daniel finished his conversation then put his phone down on the table. Heather made her way from the washroom, grabbing herself a coffee. When they were all together, Daniel looked at Elin and she nodded her head.

"Well, I guess we all felt the shaking. The all-clear siren has gone off so there is no tsunami expected," Daniel commented.

"It was a fair shaker this time," Heather added.

"That's for sure. The last one was just a tiny one. I wonder if that is an omen of things to come?" Elin asked.

"Wouldn't count on that. Each moving of the tectonic plates lets off the pressure. We haven't had a big quake for a few decades," Daniel said.

"That's true. So, what do we have to look forward to today?" Elin asked.

"Not much Elin. I'm still waiting for the paternity test results so that Roy can decide what he wants to do. I'm not sure how he feels about it all but so far, he's holding up pretty well," Heather replied.

"That's good. Will he be coming this way at all?"

"He hadn't made up his mind the last time I talked with him. I will give him a call later this morning."

"He's welcome to stay here if he wants, but our house isn't as elegant as he's accustomed to. However, the food is warm, so are the people from what I've heard."

Daniel's phone rang. He picked it up and went into the living room. They figured it must have been work, as his tone got very business-like. They had forgotten how his voice changed when he was working. He hung up then headed back into the kitchen as the home phone rang. Elin went to answer it. She made some notes on a notepad. Justin watched Daniel and Elin. He wondered if their calls had anything to do with him, or Andrew, or his mother. He felt a little stressed, but he settled himself down as he finished his coffee. Elin hung up the phone and turned towards the table.

"Well, the results from the paternity test are back. My doctor would like to discuss them with both Andrew and Roy. Do you think Roy would agree to come here? We have set up a tentative appointment for tomorrow afternoon."

Heather looked over at Elin like she was about to say something, then picked up her phone and dialled.

"Hi, Roy. It's Heather. The paternity test results are in. The doctor here would like to speak with both you and Andrew. Would you be able to be here tomorrow afternoon?"

"I see. I guess I can take the morning ferry. I'd be there by lunch time. Did he give any idea about the results?" Roy replied.

"I didn't talk with him, Elin did. However, I don't think he would ask you to be here unless there was a reason. I'm just not sure what that reason would be."

"OK. See you around lunch time. Could you please come to the doctor's office with me? I'm a little uneasy about all of this."

"For sure. Whatever the results, I will walk with you through it."

"Thanks, Heather. Even after all we have been through, you are still the best friend I have."

"That's kind of you to say. See you tomorrow."

"OK. Bye for now."

Heather hung up the phone. She turned towards Elin and Daniel. They could see the tears in her eyes and they both wondered what had been said. Justin went upstairs to get ready for his day. He was hoping to pop by Jason's to see how they were all doing, plus he wanted to see Emma. Whatever the Gray family was dealing with, they didn't need him to put his two cents in. He got his clothes together then jumped in to have a quick shower. Fancy came trotting along behind him. He figured she probably felt the tension as well.

After his shower he got dressed for the day. Then he told Elin he was heading into town to visit Jason. She gave him a hug as he left. He realised how much he appreciated the support the Gray family had given him through some of his most troubled times. He jumped in his car as he headed into town.

On his way to Jason's place, he saw Jason's car turn into the road leading to the Ravinser's property. He decided to follow it to see what was happening. He glanced at the cottage as he drove up the driveway. He was sure that he saw someone on the top floor balcony. Maybe Jason had already made it inside, but when he got closer to the house, he saw Jason and his grandpa getting out of the car. He wondered if he had really seen someone or if someone was squatting in the house since the Ravinser's went back to the mainland. He hoped that there wasn't any trouble. As he pulled up behind Jason's car, Jason turned towards him and waved. They waited until Justin parked, then headed towards his car.

"Are you following us for a reason?" Jason asked with a smile.

"No, I was just heading to your place and saw you turn in here. Can I help with anything?"

"Sure, we are just going to see if the cottage was damaged in the quake. It's not likely, but the Ravinser's want us to take a look."

"Well then an extra set of hands may be useful."

Jason opened the door as they headed inside to assess any damage. They each took a floor, grandpa did the main floor, Jason took the upper floor, and they sent Justin to the attic room.

As Justin climbed the stairs to the attic room, he thought of the times he and Emma had been up there while she was designing her outfits. She loved that room, especially being able to take breaks out on the balcony. It had the finest view of the river that Justin had ever seen. When he opened the door to the room, he smelt an odour of men's cologne and wondered where it came from. He took a quick look around the room then poked his head out on the balcony but there didn't appear to be any damage. He saw blankets and a pillow rolled up in a corner. He wondered if Emma had left those behind? As far as he could see, the attic floor was undamaged, so he headed back downstairs.

Andrew saw the men enter the house, so he slipped out the wood box door and walked through the trees to the motorway just as his phone rang. He didn't factor in that someone would check up on the cottage, so his escape had been close. He knew Justin's car. He figured the other car was Jason's. But he still didn't want them to find him in the attic room. Not only would it have been uncomfortable, but it would have meant that his new hideaway would be lost.

The property owners apparently wouldn't be returning even after the quake they had this morning. That was good to know as it meant he could still use the attic room. He would just have to be more aware if someone drove up the driveway. He had missed the first car. The minutes they chatted in the driveway gave him enough time to get out. His phone rang a second time, but he didn't recognise the phone number, so he let it go to voicemail.

He walked a little way until he found a small restaurant where he stopped to get a bite to eat. It was getting to be a daily task, to find food and a place to sleep. He was wondering if anyone saw him as homeless. He knew his mom would be horrified if she heard how he had been living. The phone rang again, it was the same number, so he didn't answer it. When he got seated in the restaurant, he went to his voicemail to see who had been calling.

The first message was from Elin Gray something about the paternity test. The next call was from Jason, telling him a little more about the results of the paternity test. It seemed like everyone knew the results but him. Apparently, he and

Roy had an appointment tomorrow afternoon with the doctor who had set up the test. He ordered his breakfast as the waiter poured him a coffee. So, where should he go from here? He needed to go home to shower. Jason had offered to pick him up to drive him to the appointment so that would be covered. He couldn't help thinking about what changes may be ahead for him. It had always been just him and his mom. For the most part, that had worked well.

His breakfast arrived and the waiter refilled his coffee. After eating, he dug in his pockets to come up with enough to cover the meal. When he went up to pay, the waitress told him that someone had already paid for his meal. He looked around the restaurant but didn't notice anyone he knew so he asked her to pass on his thanks. He headed to the washroom where he washed up. He still had enough money to take the bus home. When he left the restaurant, he headed for the bus station a block up the road. Timing was working out great as the bus pulled in just as Andrew bought his ticket. He boarded the bus, found a seat, then looked at his phone again.

The bus driver pulled away from the bus stop. Andrew placed his rucksack behind his head and closed his eyes. The bus wasn't very full, so it was quiet. Andrew nodded off. When the bus stopped Andrew opened his eyes, realising the next stop was his stop. He must have slept for a good half hour or so. He rubbed his eyes, then pulled out his phone to check for new messages. There was only one from his mother asking about when he would be home. He answered her message, then sat up putting his rucksack on the seat next to him. Today, things felt different, maybe even odd, as he considered what was going to happen at the meeting with Roy tomorrow. He felt that the results of the paternity test had been positive. That is why the two of them were meeting with the doctor, but he couldn't let himself think that way. An opposite result would then be that much harder to accept.

The bus stopped at his stop. He rose and headed for the doorway. The driver gave him a smile as he left the bus. Then he saw his mother waving at him from the side road. He smiled back at the driver as he headed towards his mom. Through everything, she was the one who had always been there. Now, he may be adding someone else into the mix. As he reached the vehicle, she opened her arms to hug him as they sat down in the vehicle.

"Good to see you home, safe and sound."

"Good to be home. I need to shower and do laundry. I have an appointment in Allerton tomorrow. Jason is going to pick me up just after lunch."

"Is it about the paternity test?"

"That is what I have been told. Got to admit I'm a little uneasy about the whole thing."

"That makes two of us. It has been just you and me for as long as I can remember."

"That is true."

Once home, he noticed that his mother had already started lunch. Even though Andrew wasn't very hungry, he sat down to eat with her. Then it was shower time, he felt so sweaty and uncomfortable. The best solution for that was a shower. He grabbed his rucksack and dropped it in his room as he continued to the washroom. The tension washed off him as he soaped up. He began to contemplate what today would hold. He was going to give Jason a call just to see what he was thinking, especially after Andrew's narrow escape from the cottage. Thinking back, he could kick himself. If he had been found in the cottage it could have messed up a lot of things. He didn't leave anything behind, but the blankets and pillow were still in the attic room. That's one reason a call to Jason would be helpful.

Jason and Austin, with Justin's help, made a thorough search of the cottage. Justin let them know about the pillow and blanket in the attic, but they didn't seem to think it was important. On their way home, Jason and Austin stopped at the grocery store as Justin waited in the car park. Within a few minutes, they came out. Justin followed them to their house. They knew he only wanted to see Emma, but they were willing to let things play out as they happened. There were no misunderstanding Justin's intentions but for now both he and Emma were keeping things cool, as this summer would be important for them both. With Justin working with Daniel at his firm and Emma finishing with her surgeries; plus, starting her design school training, there was a lot of change to plan around. Jason ran up the steps to let Emma know Justin was just behind them. It would give her enough time to do whatever she needed to do before seeing him.

Jason was starting to understand more about Rosa, about what was important to her. Austin made his way up the stairs, carrying some of the groceries they had picked up in town. Jason ran down the stairs to grab the remaining groceries from the vehicle, then headed back upstairs. His grandpa was amazing, he didn't complain about, or ask for, much. He was always looking for the solution. It occurred to Jason that his father had those same qualities. He hoped that they had been ingrained in him as well.

Justin pulled into the driveway as Emma went to the door to greet him. She was going to miss him over the summer. However, she knew that she would be busy with the surgeries and working on designs for the autumn school term. Most likely, it would make the times they could get together that much better as they would have so many new experiences to share. She was looking forward to telling Justin about the design school that she had enrolled in this morning. Its main headquarters was in the same city where Jason was taking his degree courses but most of it was online.

As Justin got to the door, her grandma came around the door of the kitchen and called everyone in for a late lunch. Justin was going to leave but Emma smiled telling him, they had put together enough for everyone. He nodded as he followed Emma into the kitchen.

When they were finishing lunch, Raymond came to the door. Jason got up to let him in, inviting him to sit down at the table with them. The grandparents told him to have lunch as well. As he hadn't eaten since breakfast, Raymond gladly accepted their offer. When they were all finished, Raymond and Jason headed upstairs. Emma and Justin decided to go for a drive while Iris and Austin cleaned off the table. Then Iris made them a cup of tea. It was nice to have some quiet time together.

Scout was barking outside so Austin went to bring him inside. Scout looked around for Emma but didn't find her, so he headed upstairs. Soon they heard Raymond and Jason talking in the hallway. They heard a door close as Scout came back downstairs followed by Ziggy. They knew that Jason was getting Raymond to redesign Alison's studio so

Emma could work out of there with her designing. Jason had made them promise to keep it secret until it was finished.

The phone rang, it was Elin looking for Justin. She had tried his phone but didn't get an answer so she figured he might be at their place. Iris told her that he and Emma had gone for a drive but should be back soon. She asked Iris to let Justin know that Daniel would be leaving the day after tomorrow so he would need to get his things together. Iris took down the message, wondering how Emma would take Justin leaving so soon. Just then, she heard Justin's car pull into the driveway.

Emma came up the stairs to the door. She turned to wave as Justin headed down the road. They had a nice drive until Elin called to tell Justin about Daniel leaving the day after tomorrow. Justin was super excited to start something new, but Emma wasn't sure how to feel about his leaving. She came inside and headed up to her bedroom to do a little designing.

Iris called out to Emma about Elin's message. Emma told her that Elin had gotten in touch with Justin. She told her grandma that Justin was heading home now, to plan what he needed to take with him when he went back with Daniel. Iris could hear the uncertainty in Emma's voice, but she knew that Emma would need some time to process what was happening in Justin's life.

Scout followed Emma into her room and jumped up on her bed. Emma cuddled him as she cried a little. Then pulling herself together, she got out her designing tablet. Scout curled up on the bed as Emma started working on an outfit. It was an evening dress with a cape. She played with the design for a few hours. Then, she began to wonder where Raymond and Jason had gone, so she went downstairs to chat a little with her grandparents. With so many transitions going on, she felt a little lonely.

When she got to the kitchen the grandparents were looking at diagrams of something. They scooped them up to make space at the table.

"What were you looking at?" Emma asked.

"Just some drawings, you know how your grandpa likes to draw things, something like you and Jason."

"That's right. I hadn't thought about that, but we do follow in grandpa's tradition."

Austin smiled over at her as Iris gave her a hug. They loved Emma and Jason so much that sometimes, there were just no words to describe it.

Chapter Nine

Andrew was up early. He began pacing around the house. He needed something to do so he grabbed a bucket as he headed outside to feed the chickens. Taking care of them was one of his favourite things to do. It was his job since he was in elementary school. First, he filled the bucket with feed, then opened the door to fill the feeding troughs. Looking around he saw that there were a lot of eggs in the nests. Gently he went over to remove the eggs. Some of the chickens gave him a rough time but his skill was well-practiced. He heard the back door open and looked up to see his mom coming towards the chicken coop. She had a bucket of vegetable peelings for the chickens. Looking at his mother, he knew that they shared the same concern over how today could change their lives.

"Are you ready for breakfast yet, Andrew?"

"You bet. What are we cooking up this morning?"

"Let's see. Scrambled eggs, toast and some fresh sliced strawberries from the grocer. Ours weren't quite ready to pick today."

"Sounds good. Can I help with anything?"

"How about you make the toast, I will scramble the eggs. The strawberries are already cut up."

They went back to the house. Andrew's phone rang so he picked it up. It was Jason so he quickly answered it.

"Hi, Jason. How's it going?"

"Not bad. I have some good news and some not so good news."

"That sounds ominous. Let's start with the bad."

"Bad news is that your appointment has been changed to 11 am so I am just on my way to pick you up."

"And the good news?"

"The good news is that Roy will make it to town just in time for the appointment."

"So, in reality it could be seen as neutral news?"

Jason laughed as he handed the phone to Justin.

"Hey, Andrew. Do you want me to come with you to the appointment?"

"Wow, that would be helpful. I could use a cheerleader today."

"OK. Jason and I will be heading out of town in a few minutes. See you soon."

"OK. Bye."

Andrew put his phone down, noticing that his mother was watching him. He looked at her and smiled. Stress filled her face as she worked on finishing her breakfast.

"My appointment has been moved up a little. Jason and Justin will be here in about an hour to pick me up."

"That's OK, right? The sooner the appointment, the sooner you will have the answers you have been looking for."

"Yes and no. I really want to know but there is a part of me that likes my life just as it is. Is that normal?"

"Extremely. This part of your life, here at home, will stay as it is. If Roy is your father, then you will be adding people to your family. That is a little scary but from what I have been able to find out, Roy is a decent sort now."

"Now? Do you mean he wasn't decent before?"

"Well, he was involved with a person who was anything but decent."

"Oh, do you mean Elliot Hayes?"

"Yes. What do you know about him?"

"Not much, just that he's Melanie's father. He died a few years back while trying to kill a member of the Gray family."

"You do know the story."

"That part, but how is Roy involved in it?"

"Roy and his wife were having difficulties. He planned to take her on a cruise on his yacht. Somehow, she ended up being kidnapped by Elliot who Roy had hired to get his yacht seaworthy. His wife suffered severe injuries, then Roy dropped out of the picture. I heard that he was having heart surgery. Nobody knew about his health problems before that as he keeps his personal life quite private. After his surgery, I'm not sure how the rest of it goes."

"So, how do you remember him, Mom?"

"We saw each other when I worked in the government office in town. He would occasionally come in to transfer title of a vehicle, or piece of property. We dated a few times, then he was off to other places. I never told him about you, so not knowing isn't his fault. I just didn't think he would want to stick around with a family."

"I get it, but didn't you ever want him to pay child support or something like that?"

"It wasn't a high priority. I had my own income, but best of all, I had you."

Andrew and his mother sat chatting about his growing years. They were good years. Both of them loved being on the farm. Growing things came as a natural part of their lives.

Andrew smiled over at his mom. All this paternity stuff couldn't be easy for her, especially today which was sort of like D-Day. He never had a father, so he didn't miss having one. Andrew recognised that he was a little headstrong, but he always thought that came from his mother. Now he wondered, if Roy turned out to be his father, what he had gotten from him.

It was getting late so Andrew ran upstairs to change into his dress clothes, such as they were. He wore his best blue jeans, a shirt, and a black denim jacket. He heard Jason's car pull into the driveway, so he ran down the stairs. Saying goodbye to his mother, he went outside to hop into the car. Jason made sure they were all buckled in, then he backed out of the driveway. They were on their way.

"Looking spiffy," Jason commented. "Is there anything you need to do before we hit Allerton?"

"I could use a coffee to travel with."

"Coffee it is," Jason said as he pulled into the rest stop. He went into the café, coming back with coffee for each of them plus a chocolate bar.

"You two need to sweeten up a bit, so here's some help," Jason said as he passed around the chocolate.

The drive to Allerton was uneventful. They mostly chatted about their plans for the summer. It was calm, but Andrew felt a little more tense with each mile. They parked at the doctor's office then went into the office. Heather and Daniel were already there, so they sat together waiting for Roy. 11 am came and he still wasn't there. The receptionist took in another patient who was also waiting to see the doctor. As they all sat watching the clock, Heather looked at her mobile phone and smiled.

"Roy has just arrived. He is outside. I'm going out to meet him," Heather said as she headed for the door.

The receptionist smiled at her. She told Heather they would be next, so Heather quickly walked outside then came right back in with Roy in hand. He looked around at the group gathered in the office lobby, wondering which one was Andrew. Looking from one of the younger men to the next, he decided he would wait until someone spoke, so he didn't make a mistake. Heather started the introductions with Elin and Daniel, Roy knew them from before, so he shook hands and smiled at them. Then Heather introduced Jason and Justin, then finally Andrew. It took Roy a minute but as he looked at Andrew, he could see his mother in him.

The receptionist took Andrew and Roy into the doctor's office. They just looked at one another not knowing what to say as the next few minutes could change everything. When the doctor came into the room, he could feel the tension in the air. He smiled at the two of them, then quickly opened a file on his desk.

"Well, this is one of the strangest appointments I have had in a long time. Thank you for trusting me with finding answers to your questions. According to the data the laboratory sent me, there is a 97% chance that you are father and son."

Andrew sat back in his chair like he was hit by a boulder. Tears slipped down his cheeks. He knew that this could be the outcome but there was still that unknown of how Roy would take the information. Roy sat straight upright in his chair, clearing his throat, trying to think of what response he should give to the doctor. He didn't have any other children. Mainly because he hadn't really wanted to have any. That was part of the reason he and Heather had difficulty in their marriage. How did you parent a young man? Would there be any room in Andrew's life for an absentee father?

"Thank you for your help, doctor." Roy said. "This is something that I never dreamed would happen to me. Today I find out I have a son. A son who has never met his father. We have lots to talk about, but I feel we just need to let it all sink in. Is that okay, Andrew?"

Andrew nodded, afraid to speak in case he started to cry again. He looked over at Roy wondering what the next step would be, and how Roy would fit in with him and his mother. Roy got up to leave. He shook the doctor's hand as Andrew opened the door to the office lobby. Five sets of eyes were peeled on him. He didn't know whether to run or sit down. Roy came out of the office, looked over at Heather and nodded. There were lots of sighs of relief, but Andrew had so many questions that it felt like things were swirling around, like in a surrealistic painting. They left the doctor's office after deciding to head to a restaurant nearby. Elin and Daniel said their goodbyes, heading home as Daniel had a lot to do before tomorrow. Justin went home with Elin and Daniel. Jason decided he would stay to have lunch with

Heather, Roy, and Andrew. In that way, he felt that Andrew would feel supported.

Justin turned on his phone when they headed home. He so wanted to talk with Emma, there had been no time to do so today. Daniel and Elin were talking about Andrew and Roy, so Justin just listened. He wasn't sure how he felt about Roy being Andrew's father, it was kind of nice when he thought that he may have a brother again. Daniel noticed that Justin had gone quiet, so he turned around to talk with him.

"Tomorrow we'll be leaving town. That is when you will begin your summer internship. After today, it may seem like a bit of a let-down, but I think you will enjoy the work. You will work with me as well as my other two partners. Elin has told me that you are good at organisation. That will be a big plus, something we need down there."

"It will definitely be an adventure. One I have been looking forward to. It would have been okay, if Andrew was my brother. I was kind of getting used to thinking that. He seemed to be doing all right with the results. In some ways, we'll always be close like brothers."

"Sometimes a close friend can be better than a brother or a sister. You are part of our family, always will be. We may not have the same parents, but we share a family bond. That is good for all of us," Elin added.

"You know what, Elin? I really do trust you and Daniel. You have offered me stability when my world got turned upside down. I will never forget that. If there is ever any way I can give back, please don't hesitate to let me know."

Elin pulled the car over to the side of the road as the tears fell from her eyes. She wiped the tears away, but

Daniel insisted on driving the rest of the way home. Before getting into the passenger seat, Elin opened the back car door to give Justin a hug. The next couple of days were going to be emotional, there was no way of changing that.

By the time they got home everyone had settled down. The next few hours would involve a lot of packing as well as saying goodbye to friends, for the summer. Justin wanted to go see his mother before he left. Elin had agreed to drive him there. It would probably not be an easy visit, but one Justin felt he needed to do.

Elin made up the extra bedroom, then put a roast in for dinner. She didn't know if Heather and Roy would be back before then, but she needed to know it was covered. Fancy followed her from room to room until Elin scooped her up to carry her to the living room sofa. The two of them sat there together. Elin braced for being alone in the house once Justin and Daniel left in the morning. She knew that Heather wouldn't stay very long but a part of her hoped she would stay for a day or two. She got up to prepare the vegetables to go in with the roast while Fancy lay under the kitchen table watching her.

Justin and Daniel were busy packing, going back and forth to see what they would need to pick up when they left tomorrow. Justin knew he needed to talk with Emma before they left but he was determined to do his packing first. He could hear Elin getting dinner started so he looked at his alarm clock and saw that time was passing quickly.

Emma sat by her phone waiting for Justin to call to let her know how things had gone. She knew that he would be busy packing as he and Daniel were leaving in the morning. Ziggy crawled up on her lap, jumping over Scout, who was laying at her feet. The phone downstairs rang. Emma got up to see if it was for her. Her grandma got to it first, by the sound of things it wasn't Justin. She went into the kitchen to grab a soda, then started up the stairs to her bedroom. Her grandma ended the phone call and joined Austin in the kitchen for a cup of tea. She asked Emma to join them, so she decided that would be better than sitting alone.

"That was your other grandma, Emma. Your grandpa had a bit of a heart incident. He is in the hospital right now. She said that it could be a little while before they would be back on the island. However, she would love it if you wanted to go over there for a visit."

Emma gasped, then closed her mouth. She couldn't imagine her life without both sets of grandparents. They were her family. The front door opened. Jason made his way into the kitchen. He looked at Emma and knew that something was going on. Grabbing a soda, he sat down at the table.

"What's going on?" Jason asked.

"Well, your other grandpa had a bit of a heart incident. He will be in the hospital for a while," Iris repeated.

"Oh, that's not good. How serious is it?"

"She didn't say much, other than letting Emma know she could come for a visit if she wanted."

"So, are you going Emma?"

"I think I'd like to be there for them like they were there for me. I'd only go for a few days as I have my surgery a week from tomorrow."

"That's right. I can take you to the ferry in the morning. Then grandma, or one of her siblings, could pick you up on the other side."

"That would work. Is that okay with you and grandpa?"

"Do what you need to do, Emma. We'll be here when you get back."

"Thanks," Emma said as she went upstairs to begin packing. She sent a text message to Justin about going to the mainland. Then she remembered that she needed to let her grandma know she would be coming. She went downstairs but Iris had already made the arrangements with the other grandma, so Emma headed back upstairs. Jason sauntered upstairs with Ziggy riding on his shoulder and Scout following behind him. He looked in at Emma to see if she was doing all right. He couldn't believe how much she had grown up since the last time he had been home.

"Emma, I just talked with Rosa. She wants to be there with you when you have your surgery. You've made a good friend in Rosa. She loves you like a little sister."

"I care a lot for her, too. Is she going to be my sister-in-law?" Emma asked with a giggle.

Jason turned around, heading back down to the kitchen. Emma was going to be okay.

When he got to the kitchen, grandma and grandpa were looking over the drawings again. Jason went over to peek at them too. He was determined to build Emma a design studio where their mother's art studio once was. It was the perfect size with the right lighting. Grandpa looked up at him, giving him a thumbs up. The drawings were well done.

Raymond was scheduled to start the renovations next week. They would continue while Emma was in having her surgery. Raymond had asked Casey to help him, so with the two of them, and grandpa supervising, it should come together quickly. They were hoping to buy some of the necessary furnishings, but they needed to get a better look at the space after the renovations. They decided it would also be wise to wait until Emma could help choose what would work in her space. They heard the washroom door close, so they rolled up the plans, putting them back in the desk drawer.

Emma came down the stairs, looking at the three of them in the kitchen. She got that feeling that something was going on. As she got closer to the kitchen, Iris and Austin started working on dinner. Scout was following Emma, but he whimpered a little, so she turned around to see Ziggy playing with his tail. She picked up Ziggy, giving him a few pets, then turned him over to Jason. Scout immediately left the room and headed for the living room sofa. Ziggy climbed up on Jason's shoulder where he started purring. Jason was going to miss Ziggy when he went back to school.

The phone rang so Emma went to answer it. It was her other grandma just confirming that Emma was coming her way. She wanted to let Emma know, she would be picked up at the ferry terminal by her and her younger sister. When Emma hung up, she realised how little time she had to get everything in order. She headed back up to her bedroom to finish organising everything for her trip to the mainland. As well as all that, she decided to begin to plan what sort of things she would need when she went in for her surgery.

Her phone rang. It was Justin calling to let her know he was going for a quick visit with his mother. He wondered if she would like to go for a drive before they each went their separate ways tomorrow. Emma winced a little but agreed to a short drive as it could be several weeks before they saw each other again. She sorted her clothing into a couple of piles, then started packing her suitcase. Her tablet with its charger, and her phone charger lay on top of the clothing in the suitcase. The tablet was getting older, but it was the one her dad bought for her after the car crash. It was her assistant all through high school. Now it was just part of who she was. Jason came down the hallway to tell her that dinner was ready. Scout was already waiting for her at the bottom of the stairs.

"Well, it's great to see everyone sit around the same table. I guess it will be a while before we do this again with Jason heading back to school tomorrow. Jason, could you please give thanks for the food?" their grandma asked.

"Thank you for this food and for the people who are gathered around this table." Everyone looked up as they started in on their meal. Emma was starting to feel a little pressured, so she needed to talk some things out.

"I'm going to go for a short drive with Justin after dinner. We won't see each other for a few weeks so it will be our goodbye."

"That will be a little different but you both will be really busy," her grandma added.

"I know, Grandma. It's just that so much is going on right now. Sometimes I feel like I don't even have time to think."

"Just take it one day at a time. It will all come together."

Elin and Justin headed down the motorway to the Mental Health Recovery Centre. Justin was trying to think out how he would tell his mother that he was going to be away for the summer. He didn't know what kind of effect it would have on her, if any, but he wanted to make sure he did it well, so she knew he loved her. He wished that he had talked more to Elin about it, but he had been busy packing to leave in the morning. The centre came in sight. Elin signalled and turned into the car park. She parked a little way from the door, so he was able to take some deep breaths before going in. Once he got to the reception desk, he asked to see his mother. The receptionist looked at him like he was green or something.

"Mrs. Knowles is resting now. Can you come back later?"

"No, not really. I'm leaving for work down island for the summer. I just wanted to have a quick chat with her so I could let her know."

"Hold on, I'll call her attendant."

The receptionist dialled a number, then told whoever was on the other end of the line that Mrs. Knowles' son was here. She looked up at Justin as she put the phone back down. The attendant approached the desk, so the receptionist introduced Justin to her. They went to a tiny office where the attendant gently closed the door.

"It's Justin, right?"

"Yes."

"Justin, when your mother came back in recently, she was not totally coherent. She has been under full medication for several days. Right now, she is resting but I can take you down to her room. You can tell her as much as you consider necessary. She may be awake but I'm not sure how much she will comprehend."

"OK. I would like to let her know about me being away for a while. I will keep it simple but will leave my number at reception if she wants to talk with me at any time."

"That sounds good. I think it would be best if I stayed with you."

"That is fine. You know all the skeletons already, so I have no problem with you being present."

At that, the attendant opened the door. They headed down the hallway to his mother's room. He looked through the window on the door before they entered the room. He saw that his mother was resting peacefully. For that, he was grateful. He walked into the room then gently took her hand in his. She moved a little, but she still appeared to be sleeping. He took a few minutes to tell her about his job down island as well as how he would be back after his summer internship was over. It was important to Justin that she knew he was just a phone call away. He told her he was leaving his phone number at reception if she ever wanted to chat. After giving her a gentle kiss on the forehead, he headed back out the door.

"Justin."

Justin turned around but his mother was still sleeping. The attendant smiled at him. She told him his mother must have understood what he told her. He left the centre feeling good that he had gone ahead with the visit, even while she was resting. Once he got back home, he jumped in his car to head over to Emma's. Saying goodbye to everyone was not easy.

Chapter Ten

Andrew pulled himself out of bed then slowly started to the washroom. After yesterday, he was uncertain what today would bring. He felt uneasy, yet excited at the same time. He went back to his bedroom to dress before going downstairs for breakfast, even though the smell of fresh coffee wafted up to his room. He looked outside to see the sun etching through the morning fog. It looked almost magical with the dew shining on the plants. It was already 9 am, so he knew that his mother would have already fed the chickens.

Galloping down the stairs he landed in the kitchen with a smile. His mother looked over at him. It was the same today as it was yesterday, as it had been many yesterdays before then. They both knew that today could change their entire world, but his mother was determined to stick to the routine they had both counted on to make it this far. Today, she would see Roy Ahns after 17 years. She had no idea what to say to him. She wasn't sorry for keeping Andrew's birth quiet. Hopefully, that wouldn't be a point of contention. There was nothing that she wanted from Roy, not money, nor companionship, nor anything at all. She was wondering if he could accept that. Truthfully that is what made her a little apprehensive. His ex-wife, Heather, was going to accompany him. She wondered if that was the smartest move as well. When she felt backed into a corner, Marley's first instinct was to fight. That would not be productive at all.

Marley cleaned up the breakfast dishes as she started planning the lunch that she would be serving Roy and his entourage. It would be simple, but delicious. She decided to start with a fresh green salad made with some of the ingredients from her garden. Then she was going to make sandwiches with home-made bread. She was thinking egg salad, tuna, as well as ham and cheese. Then for dessert, there would be fresh strawberries from her garden with a shortcake base as well as some whipped cream, or maybe she'd do up some chocolate-dipped strawberries. She got Andrew to go pick the first strawberries from their garden as well as lettuce and green onions, while she boiled up some eggs.

Feeling the need to keep busy, Marley decided to do some cleaning. She grabbed the vacuum, cleaning the carpet and floors. It would just be the four of them, but she needed to make a good impression. She wanted to prove to Roy, and his companion, that she was a good mother as well as a good provider.

Once the floors dried, she headed to the kitchen to make up the salad and start preparing the dessert. She decided to keep dessert to the strawberries on the shortcake base. Once done with that, she made the filling for the sandwiches and put it in the fridge until just before the guests arrived. The newly opened loaf of bread was waiting on the counter.

Marley contemplated what dishes to use, as her good set rarely made it out of the cabinet. Just to notch it up a little she removed the tablecloth from the table, putting on a cloth that she had bought from a local artisan. It was beautiful, reminding her of the nature that surrounded her. Then came the dishes, a white ensemble with small little roses around the rims of the plates. They had belonged to her mother but somehow it felt comforting to use them today. She finished setting the table, then went upstairs to decide what to wear. She decided to keep it casual, so she chose a leisure suit. Looking at the clock she went back downstairs, put on her apron, and began to finish preparing the lunch.

She had just finished the sandwiches when Andrew came downstairs to tell her that they were just a few minutes away. Andrew went to the door to usher them in as well as make the introductions. Marley looked at Roy. She was astonished at how different he looked from when she knew him. She wondered how she stacked up to the memories he had of her. His companion, Heather, was gracious. Marley was taken aback by her gentle kindness.

"Welcome to our home." Marley said as she brought them into the dining room. "Take whatever seat you would like, we're not fussy."

"You have a beautiful property here," Heather said.

"It belonged to my parents. It became mine many years ago. I love it, always have. We grow a lot of our own food. I have a few chickens as well."

"Mom, would you like me to help bring out the food?"

"Thanks, Andrew. Could you please bring in the water and juice."

"Can do. Roy, it must seem odd meeting my mother after all these years?"

"It has been quite a long time. You look beautiful as always, Marley."

"Thanks. I'm sure we have both changed a lot over the last couple of decades."

Andrew and Marley took their seat next to each other as Heather and Roy sat together on the other side of the table. It felt awkward but Andrew was determined to make it all work out. They finished their lunch, then Andrew took them into the living room where they could chat. He had a lot of questions, but he was aware that his mother probably felt a little uneasy, so he asked Roy about how he was doing. That led to the tale of his boat and Heather being kidnapped. Roy touched Heather's hand while he spoke. She just smiled at him.

"So, Andrew, tell me a little about yourself. I believe you have finished or are finishing high school, have you any plans for the next stage of your life?" Roy asked.

"Not really. I've considered a few careers but haven't made any solid plans. At one point I was going to be a fisher. That turned into maybe manufacturing seafood into food products that could be sold locally and abroad."

"There is a local seafood company, have you tried getting on with them? It would be the best way to learn the business," Roy added.

"I have. I applied a few days back for the upcoming summer season. They said they would get back to me within a week or so."

"If I can help in any way, let me know, OK?"

"OK. I'm thinking of taking some business courses online, while I am working this summer. Do you recommend any school?"

"Not really. Courses in finance, HR, and marketing would all be helpful."

Heather looked over at Marley. She could see that Marley felt a little left out, so she asked her to show her the garden. They got up and went outdoors. Heather saw the chickens, smiling at how organised everything was out there. She remembered that Marley had worked as the government agent so being organised would have been necessary. They sauntered back to the house where they saw that Andrew and Roy were still talking away. Heather helped Marley put together tea then they took it into the living room. Neither Andrew nor Roy looked upset or uneasy, so it seemed like their talk had gone well. When they finished their tea, both Heather and Roy began getting ready to leave.

"Marley, if you need anything, anything at all, please let me help. I owe you so much. Andrew is an amazing young man."

"He has worked pretty hard to get where he is."

Roy went over to hug Andrew, so Heather gave Marley a hug. Then Roy and Heather were on their way.

When they turned onto the motorway to head back to Allerton, they sat without really saying too much. They were both deep in thought. It felt comfortable to be there for now. Heather turned towards Roy. She watched him as he tried to put all the pieces together. Then she realised, he would be thinking about how to make everything right. She and Roy had discussed having children many times during their marriage, but he always had other plans. She waited to feel some sort of distaste or sadness, but it never came.

She loved watching Andrew and Roy together when they were just chatting. She was amazed at how they sometimes talked about things in a similar manner. Heather liked Marley, even though she kept Andrew's birth from Roy. She understood why Marley may have thought that would work better all around. But today was a new day. Heather wondered what the next step would be as well as wondering if it would involve her in any way.

Roy turned into a rest area. He sat there for a few moments before he turned to Heather.

"So, what do you think, Heather?"

"I think you have a remarkable son. I like his mother. She expects nothing from you, not now or ever."

"Does that make it all right?"

"It depends on what you are talking about. I think the best path is to take today as day one, then go on from there or you have the possibility of losing what you have gained."

"But you always wanted children. I wasn't always at the same place that you were."

"I know. Do I regret not having kids? Probably a part of me does, but that shouldn't stop you from having a relationship with your son."

"I'll need to make some changes to my life, including finding somewhere to stay close by but far enough away to give Andrew and his mother space."

"That's a good thought. We can look into what is available in Allerton as well as the surrounding area."

“Yes, that would be a good place to start. I told Andrew we could meet for coffee tomorrow afternoon. Can you please come along with us?”

“Sure, but is it necessary? You two seem to get along well.”

“We do. How about if you and Elin have coffee at the same time, same restaurant?”

Heather giggled. “Sure, that works for me. I haven’t had a lot of time with Elin. Now that Daniel and Justin have gone back to work, she may have some free time.”

“Then that’s a plan. We can talk with Elin when we get back home. Can we pick up some dinner when we get back to town, so Elin doesn’t have to cook?”

“Good idea. I will give her a call to find out if she has already planned something.”

Heather called up Elin. When Heather hung up, she looked over at Roy.

“Too late Roy, Elin already has a feast for us for dinner. We can do the dinner thing tomorrow if you want.”

“Tomorrow works for me. You know I really love your family. Both Daniel and Elin are incredibly kind people. Hopefully, I will grow up to become more like them.”

“I think you are already on that path. Just hang in there. How are you feeling?”

“Good. A little tired but that will pass. Tonight, it will be dinner, shower and bed.”

“Sounds good. Let’s pick up some dessert at the bakery, it will be our contribution.”

Roy headed back onto the motorway. There wasn’t much traffic, so it was an easy drive and time flew by quickly. When they hit town, they stopped at the bakery to get an assortment of baked goods to add to the feast. Heather got a text from Daniel, telling her he was back in the capital. He hoped things went well with Roy and Andrew. She messaged him back to give him a brief update.

Roy's boat was being brought around to the marina in the next few days, so he stopped in there to make sure his space was ready. He was back in a few minutes with a smile, everything was good. They finished the drive to Elin's place. Elin was still working on the feast, so Heather and Roy went to change before dinner.

It had been an interesting day for Elin. Justin had just sent her a text to tell her he was at Daniel's. He told Elin that he would miss her, and she started to cry. Too many days alone would not be easy for Elin. Justin promised to keep in touch. She knew that he and Daniel would be back in town often to look at the new office complex Daniel's company was building.

Justin sat in his room as the exhaustion of the day rolled over him. Tomorrow would be his first day at work. He was both excited and a little scared. He looked at his phone to see if Emma had sent him a message yet, but there was none. He knew that the ferry had just landed so it may take a bit to get through the depot.

Emma walked off the ferry on the mainland. She looked around for her grandma. She really was looking forward to spending some time with her. Justin was away for the summer, so her summer would be different this year. Looking around the various vehicles that drove by, she didn't see either grandmother or her sister. Taking out her phone, she dialled her grandma's number, and she answered right away.

“Sorry, my dear. We are caught in a bit of traffic, we should be there soon.”

“Thanks, Grandma. I was just a little worried.”

“Give us ten minutes and we’ll be driving around the pickup lanes.”

“See you soon. Love you.”

“Love you, too, Emma.”

Emma found a bench to sit on, thankful that things were going as planned. While waiting for her grandma, she decided to text Justin to see if they had made it to Daniel’s place. He had been a little apprehensive about staying there, but Emma assured him that Daniel’s wife and daughters were just like Daniel. They liked to kid around a lot and have fun. Justin messaged her back a picture of Daniel’s house with the party they had set up for when he and Daniel reached home this afternoon. He also sent her a picture of the whole family, plus him. He was smiling. That was going to work well for the summer, although, Emma wondered if he would want to come back home after that, or maybe stay down there. Anyway, she wasn’t going to think about anything but today. So far, today was awesome.

A car with its headlights flashing was coming her way. She saw that grandma’s sister was driving. They honked a couple of times, Emma picked up her suitcase and rucksack to head to the car. Grandma got out to give her a big hug, thanking her for coming to stay for a little while. Emma asked about grandpa. She was told he was in the hospital for observation, but they hoped he would be home in a few days. They started to find their way out of the pickup zone as they headed for the motorway.

Emma messaged her other grandparents to let them know she had arrived safe and sound on the mainland. She told them she was in the car with the other grandma. Iris messaged her back, sending her a big hug. Even though Emma still missed her parents, she was grateful for her grandparents. She realised that taking care of her and Junior meant that they lost out on things like travelling or taking advantage of their retirement time.

It took a little time, but they finally reached her grandma's house. Emma insisted on carrying her own suitcase and rucksack, so the two sisters grabbed the groceries from the boot car. It looked like they had done quite a bit of shopping before picking her up. Emma put her suitcase and rucksack in the foyer then headed back out to the car to help carry in groceries.

Once that was done, she looked at her grandma. Her grandma told her to head down the hallway to her old room. When she got there, she saw the bed made up with some of her favourite chocolate put on the bedside table. She unpacked her suitcase then stretched out on the bed for a few minutes. The next thing she knew, grandma was in her room shaking her arm to wake her up, supper was on the table.

Emma got up and went to the washroom to freshen up a bit. How long had she been sleeping? She had to admit that the last few weeks had been packed with so many things. Maybe she truly needed this break to get ready for her upcoming surgery. As she made her way to the kitchen, she could hear the two sisters chatting about what they had planned for tomorrow. Emma really wanted to go see her grandpa. She heard the two sisters saying that he was looking forward to seeing her.

Emma also wanted to do a little shopping at some of the upscale shops to see what was trending in fashion in this region. Looking at fashion, then seeing what she could change, such as a different fabric, or cut of a dress, made her creativity come alive.

After dinner, Emma sat with the two ladies in the living room while they watched the evening news. Then grandma's sister got up to head home for the night. She made sure to let Emma know that they had a full day planned for tomorrow. Emma thanked her for everything. Grandma and Emma sat together to watch some TV. Then her grandma said she was a little tired. Emma understood that grandma was heading to bed for the night. She helped turn off the lights and made sure the doors were locked. In a way, Emma was glad that her grandma was calling it a night as she felt incredibly tired herself.

As Emma got ready for bed, she had to admit that she missed having Scout and Ziggy around, but she knew the other grandparents would look after them. She pulled out her tablet to look at the design that she had been working on. It was a surprise but also a bit of wishful thinking as she had started to design Rosa's wedding dress. This trip would give her a chance to check out some of the wedding shops to see what was popular. She wanted to incorporate some style elements to make something original for her future sister-in-law. She made a few adjustments to the dress, then added some extra beading on the bodice. Then she erased the beading to add sequins instead. Neither look made her happy, so she closed the tablet and lay down.

Jason received the text from Emma letting him know that she had landed on the mainland. He sent her a short text back, telling her he was at the university. Emma sent him a smiley face then turned off her phone.

When Jason opened the door to his flat, it smelled like something had been cooking in the oven. He quickly put down his suitcase as he hurried into the kitchen. It was empty but there was a note on the oven that said there was some lasagna in the oven. It should be ready to eat around 6 pm. He smiled as he realised that Rosa had been in to make him dinner. He wondered if she would be joining him, so he quickly took his suitcase into his room. Then he transferred his computer from the rucksack to his office which was just a corner in the living room. He set it all up, then took out his phone to call Rosa.

"Hi, Jason. Are you back in town?"

"Yes, took Emma to the ferry, then stopped at the university. After that I headed straight home. Tomorrow I will be back in class, so I've got tonight to finish unpacking. Thank you for the amazing dinner. Will you be joining me?"

"I have an evening class, but I can come after that."

"What time does it end?"

"It goes from 5:30 pm to 7 pm. Would that be too late?"

"I can wait until then. I have some biscuits that my grandma sent me back with, so I can have a snack. We can eat together."

"Looking forward to that. We can catch up at the same time."

"OK. See you later."

"Bye."

Jason hung up the phone as he opened the care package his grandma had sent home with him. He couldn't help smiling. He grabbed a couple of biscuits, made himself a cup of coffee and headed into his office. Maybe he could get some of his assignment done before dinner.

The oven timer went off, so Jason went into the kitchen to put it back on the warming cycle. He brought out garlic bread from the freezer. Looking out his window, he saw the traffic on the motorway. He wondered how grandpa Ravinser was doing. He went back into the living room to sit down at his desk as he began looking around at different companies he was interested in. A part of him wanted to make sure that wherever he went, Rosa would feel comfortable. But then there was that longing to return to Allerton. He only had a few months to figure it all out.

A few companies had approached him, as the university was one of the resources companies used to find staff. From what he could understand so far, one of them was looking for someone to work on the island while another one was looking for someone who was willing to travel. Both positions were alluring as they offered different experiences. He hadn't talked to his grandparents about any of that as he needed to figure it out himself before looking for any input. If he travelled a lot, it would mean less time with family, but it would give him a whole new insight into the occupation he was entering.

His phone rang. He saw it was his grandpa, so he quickly picked up.

"Hi, Jason. Just checking that you made it home safely. We've already heard from Emma. She's doing well on the mainland."

"I'm at home. Just waiting for Rosa to come over. She made us a lasagna for dinner. Actually, she made me a lasagna, but I asked her to join me."

"Oh. It's a little late for dinner but I'm sure you have stuff to snack on. I saw what my wife put into the tin that she gave you."

"Yes, I had a late afternoon coffee break. I am just heading to the kitchen to put the garlic bread in the oven."

"Well, I won't keep you. We loved having you home for a spell. Hopefully, we can do more of that."

"That's the plan. I'm working through the summer to finish early. Classes should be completed by the end of July."

"Then we can plan our next big graduation party. Have a good night."

"You too, Grandpa. Love you both."

"Love you too."

Jason hung up his phone and sat in the quiet for a few moments. He was having one of those days, where he missed his parents. But he was smart enough to realise that at each transition he would miss talking with his dad. Looking at his family pictures, he realised that time could heal a lot of the hurt, but the longing remained. The doorbell rang so he went to answer it. Looking through the window, he saw it was Rosa.

Chapter Eleven

Iris and Austin sat watching the evening news, gearing down for the night. It had been an extremely busy couple of weeks. Tomorrow Raymond would be starting on Emma's studio. Iris made their nightly tea and took the tray into the living room. Austin looked up smiling. She could see that he looked tired as well. They had their tea, then Austin turned off the TV and closed the curtains. Iris turned off the lights as she followed him upstairs. A week without any kids would be unusual but they could use that time to figure out their next step. They fell asleep thinking about the grandkids, wondering what the next couple of weeks would bring.

It was still dark when Iris woke to the sound of a siren. She gently rolled over and saw that Austin was still sleeping. Quietly, she went to the window to look out. All she could see was a few streetlights. The siren was still going off, then their mobile phones started to beep. That is when Austin woke up and looked over at her. It took her a few minutes to realise that it was the tsunami warning system, but the regular test was still a few days away; plus, it was always in the afternoon. She headed downstairs as Austin grabbed his robe. Scout was howling while Ziggy was hiding behind the sofa in the living room. She turned on the light, then the TV, to see if she could find any information.

At first there was only the regular programming but then a newscaster broke in. He reported that the west coast was on tsunami alert as there was a large earthquake up north. Austin looked at his mobile phone, finding the earthquake app that Jason had added to his phone. He looked at what was posted about the size of the earthquake. It had been read as a 7.5 which is considered an earthquake that could cause a tsunami. They made a pot of coffee as they sat and watched the newscaster report what they knew about the quake so far. There was damage to the cities closer to the epicentre, but so far there was no reported wave. Vehicles started to move on the roads, but Iris and Austin knew that where they sat, they were out of harm's way.

Iris got them blankets to curl up in. Then they sat up in front of the TV watching the reporting on the earthquake. Apparently, there was a small wave started but it was only about a foot and half high. They were asking people to avoid the river front area, telling them not to gather to watch the wave come in. Austin shook his head as he wondered how anyone would want to head towards something that had been classified as a potential hazard. As the hours rolled by, the danger level was lowered. Both Austin and Iris fell asleep in their recliners. Ziggy jumped up to cuddle with Iris as Scout sat between the two chairs watching daybreak over the mountains.

The phone rang. Austin woke up and grabbed for the portable phone that they had put between them.

"Grandpa, are you and grandma, okay?" Emma asked.

"We are good, dear. Nothing came of the earthquake, thank goodness. How are you and Ruby doing?"

"We slept through most of it. That is up until the mobile phones got their alert going."

"Well, I guess it's another day to be thankful for, do you have any plans for today?"

"Apparently the two sisters have the day all planned out. Tell grandma I love her and miss her. Same for you, Grandpa."

"We miss you too. Enjoy your day."

"OK. Bye for now."

"Bye."

Austin hung up the phone. He looked over at Iris who was just getting up from her chair.

"That was Emma, she was just checking in. She told me to tell you that she loves you and misses you."

"Aww, that's sweet. I kind of miss the noisy household we had gotten used to."

"Well, it should be noisy today. Raymond is due to start at 9 am, which is half an hour from now."

"We better grab some breakfast then. Can you check on Jason?" Iris asked.

"Can do. I think I will get dressed first."

"Sounds good. Me, too."

Iris dressed while Austin was calling Jason. She listened in to the conversation. Everything was fine with Jason, although he, too, had been awakened by a tsunami warning siren. Austin finished his conversation as Iris headed downstairs to start the coffee. She felt a little more tired than usual but not enough to stop her from doing what needed to be done. Scout followed her to the kitchen, so Iris took him out to his dog run/kennel for a jaunt before starting the day. Ziggy sat at the window near the back door and watched them until she heard Austin get her food out of the cupboard. She made it to the kitchen in no time at all. From the looks of the sky, it was going to be a beautiful day out. Iris began to think about the garden and about getting the lawn mowed. However, it wasn't going to be a priority today, as the renovations would be all that was important for now.

A pickup truck pulled up in front of the house with Raymond following behind it. He unloaded the lumber, carrying most of it up to Alison's studio to start the renovation. Austin made his way outside to see what was happening. Raymond looked over at him and smiled.

"So, you made it through the sirens last night, did you?"

"Yes. It was a little unnerving, but I know we are above the inundation zone."

"Mom slept all the way through it. She needs to have her hearing retested, besides she doesn't wear her hearing aids at night."

"We could make something that pulsed on her pillow if the sirens went off. It would take a little designing, but Jason and I could spend some time working on it. With all that you have helped us with, it would be nice to help you for a change."

"Truthfully, we would appreciate any help you could give. This hearing thing is getting pretty serious."

"I'll talk with Jason today. We'll get it started. It will be good to have something to work on with the kids both away for most of the summer."

Raymond smiled as he started to move all the furniture out of the studio. They had decided to give the furnishings away, so there was pickup truck coming this afternoon to pick it up. Elin had mentioned to Raymond that she was looking for shelf units, so he looked through the things they were taking out. Once the furniture was out, Raymond could start working on the space where Emma's desk would be. They wanted to take lighting into consideration as it appeared that Emma liked working in the evening. Also, while she was doing classes there would often be late nights. He started framing in her desk as Austin came to the door. He invited Raymond downstairs for some lunch. Time was going by quickly, but lunch sounded good. It would give him time to discuss a few of the design features that were on the plans. He also gave Elin a call to tell her that there were a couple shelf units that she may be interested in. They had left them on the front porch for her. She told Raymond that she would pay him for delivery, if that was possible. Raymond said he could deliver them after work, no charge.

Elin and Fancy sat in the kitchen feeling the quietness deeply. She loved having a full house. Now the only other people left at the house were Heather and Roy. She missed Justin. It had been a tradition with her parents that their house would always be a place for young people who were struggling.

Roy and Heather hadn't mentioned when they would be leaving but she thought they probably wouldn't stick around long, as they both had places on the mainland. She knew they were considering a lot of things, now that Roy had found out that Andrew was his son.

Hearing footsteps she looked up to see Heather coming into the kitchen. Elin had to admit that Heather looked happy this morning. She wondered what was up. Another set of footsteps came into the kitchen. Fancy jumped up to greet Roy as he grabbed a cup to pour himself a coffee.

"Looks like Fancy prefers you over me, Roy. Have you been sneaking her treats?" Heather joked.

"No, not at all. She just isn't used to having me around."

"So, what are your plans for today?" Elin asked them both.

"Well, it's a little complicated. I'd like to find a house or property so I would have a place here where I could visit with Andrew."

"Interesting. Anywhere in particular?"

"I'd love to be near the water, somewhere I could build a dock for my boat."

"You heard the sirens last night, right?" Elin asked.

"Yes, but that is pretty common for here, at least that is what Heather told me."

"It seems to be getting more common each day. Most of the riverside properties are in the inundation zone."

"So that means I should be able to buy something fairly inexpensively, no?"

"That's one way to look at it," Elin replied with a giggle.

Fancy jumped up a few times until Roy picked her. Elin pulled some cinnamon buns and fruit out of the fridge as she put out plates for Roy and Heather. Heather jumped up to help but Elin told her to finish her coffee. Elin's phone dinged. She looked at it to see who was calling. Apparently, there was a fishery opening tomorrow so she had some things to check out before tomorrow.

"Well, folks, I am heading to my boat to see what needs to be done before tomorrow. Feel free to come and go as you need to. I think that the Ravinser's may be putting their property up for sale. They have become a little restless since Emma graduated, especially with Emma moving back to her family home."

"Thanks for the tip. We will take a look at the property. We'll also supply dinner tonight, so you just do whatever needs to be done to your boat."

"Thanks, Heather. Come on, Fancy, let's go for a drive."

Fancy jumped down from Roy's lap to follow Elin out to her vehicle. They arrived at the car park, then walked down the ramp to her boat. She loved being on her boat so she took her time to go through all the supplies as well as other things she would need for tomorrow. There were a few things that she needed to pick up. She decided to start a list. She heard footsteps behind her, so she turned around. Casey was coming down the dock with a big smile on his face.

"Knew I would find you here today. Do you need a helper for tomorrow?"

"I could always use help; I could even give you some of the fish if you want to help."

"Sounds good. Gave my last one to my folks last week. How have you been doing? It's been a while since we chatted?"

"Doing well. Lots of stuff going on. I guess you have been busy between working and helping your folks with the changes to their house."

"Uh huh. The renovations should be finished this week, which I am grateful for. I like being able to help them, but I need some time to just relax a little, fishing helps me do that."

"Wow, sounds like you are getting all Zen on me, Casey. Are you OK?"

"OK, yes. Elin, I miss spending time with you. Would you like to come out for dinner with me tonight?"

"Thanks for the invite, Casey, but Heather and Roy are preparing dinner for us tonight. Would you like to join us?"

"No, I don't think so. Maybe on the weekend we could do dinner?"

"I will keep it open for a dinner with you. How's work going at the seafood factory?"

"Excellent. Received another promotion, even though I don't think I really did anything to get it."

"Congrats! You must have shown them that you are dependable and capable. That is a tough combination to find today."

"Maybe. I do like working down there. It's like basketball, once the fish are processed and packaged, you have made a basket. The more of those you do a night, the better it feels."

"Sounds like you've found your niche. I'm not sure I know this Casey."

"Same old Casey. Just a little older and today, a little more tired."

"Yah, I guess everyone slept a little less last night with the warning siren blaring."

"For sure. However, it was also exciting. From what I could find out, there were no fatalities linked to the earthquake so that is a plus. Then a two-foot wave is almost non-existent. However, I heard some people gathered along the river to see the wave."

"That was okay for this time but if a larger wave happens there will be no time to run if you are waiting at the river to see it."

"True. Looks like you're finished, do you want to go for a coffee?"

"Could do. But can it be at a food truck, so Fancy doesn't get stuck in the car?"

"Sure, meet you at the marina."

"See you there."

Elin and Fancy got into her vehicle as they headed towards the marina. It had been quite some time since she and Casey had spent any time together which made Elin feel a little anxious. After completing her recovery programme Elin was determined to stay clean and sober. Casey felt that her determination came off as if he were being judged so things cooled between the two of them. Right now, she was just meeting an old friend for a coffee, nothing more and nothing less. Fancy barked from her kennel. Elin looked around to see that she was scratching at the kennel's floor. She wasn't used to being put in it, so she was letting Elin know she didn't like it. It was just a short jaunt to the marina. Elin turned on the car radio to listen to some music.

As she pulled into the car park, some of the memories came flooding back…Trevor's death…Alison's art show…Heather's kidnapping. Elin took Fancy out of her crate and put on her leash. Casey was already waiting by the food truck. Fancy was ready to go so they jogged towards him.

"Beautiful day today, not the typical morning after," Elin started.

"True. But living on the coast we get used to the warnings, and the shaking, every once in a while. It's a small price to pay to live on this side of paradise."

"That it is, can't wait to get out fishing tomorrow. I swear the coastal mountains and waterways get more enticing each time the fishing season starts."

"I'm not sure about enticing, but definitely exciting. Heard Heather and Daniel were visiting, is your company all gone now?"

"Daniel has gone home. He took Justin with him as well. Justin will intern with his firm this summer. Heather is still here, so is Roy."

"Roy? Now that's a name I haven't heard in a while."

"He's looking for property near here. That is why they are making dinner tonight."

"Sounds good. It must feel good to have a night off once in a while."

"It is, but I'll miss having Justin around this summer. He has been living at the house for a lot of years. He's become a very real part of our family."

"Hmm. I almost envy that."

"Let's see, there is coffee, hot chocolate, herbal tea or a soda. What are you going to get?" Elin asked as she skirted around his comment.

"I'm going to take the hot chocolate, and you?"

"Make it two hot chocolates, please."

Casey gave the order to the food truck worker and waited for the hot chocolates as Elin found them a table. A part of Casey wanted to kick himself as he had just got to the point where he was okay without Elin. Now, he was starting it all over again. It felt good yet scary at the same time.

As Casey got closer to the table, Fancy started jumping up and down. He put the drinks down on the table as he remembered how he always was well-loved by that dog. She looked up at him in such an irresistible manner that he had to bend down to give her a cuddle. However, she jumped into his arms, so he sat down, holding her as she licked his face. Elin started to laugh as she took a picture on her mobile phone. All the tension passed as Fancy took her place on the bench next to Casey.

Elin and Casey decided to take Fancy for a walk along the river walkway, as the weather was warm. It would also give them time to discuss tomorrow's fishery. Casey knew that Elin would want to get an early start to miss all the other traffic on the river. When they finally got back to the car park, all the details had been worked out. They said their goodbyes as they went their separate ways. Elin was unsure of where it was all going but she was smart enough to know to take one small step at a time. A good friendship would be better than an acrid relationship. She put Fancy back in her kennel then headed home as it was getting close to dinner time. She wondered how Roy was at putting together a meal; however, she knew Heather was good at such things.

Roy and Heather were busy putting together the evening meal. It was easy when they used all the local shops where they had found some delicious entrees. Then fresh vegetables, fruit, and finally pastries from a local bake shop. Heather was surprised that Roy seemed to enjoy the prepping and cooking. When Elin pulled into the driveway, they were just putting the rice in a bowl and dishing up the different entrees. They cooked enough for a small army, but they knew whatever was left could be warmed up later. Maybe, in some small way, that would help Elin. When the front door opened, Fancy bounded in, heading for the kitchen. She jumped up on them until they gave her a pet. Elin headed for the washroom, then came back to help with the dinner. By then, the table was all set with the food. She looked at the table and gasped.

"Wow. When you guys prepare a feast, you really mean a feast."

"It's definitely a feast. Whatever is left you can freeze for later. Roy and I have had a good day so it's truly a celebration."

"Did you find the property you were looking for?"

"Not exactly. But we've put out feelers. We were told that there would be several properties coming on the market in the next month," Roy explained.

"That is good news. Just a question, you don't have to answer. Will you both be moving, temporarily, back to town?"

"We did a little talking about that but haven't quite made a plan yet. You will be one of the first to know," Heather answered.

"OK. That's it for my questions. Let's dig in, this smells wonderful."

They each chatted about their day as Fancy hung out under the table, jumping up on Elin when she had finished her meal. Elin put her down as she started helping to clean off the table. When the dishes were all at the sink, Roy and Heather told her to go watch TV as they would do the clean-up. Elin wandered into the living room and turned on the TV. It was news time, so she watched the local evening news then headed to her room. She heard a phone ring in the kitchen and then heard Roy make his way to the living room.

"Hi, Asher, have you got good news?"

"Some. We should be ready to head to the other side of the island tomorrow. Have you found a spot for us yet?" Asher replied.

"For sure. I'm also looking at some property. Could you look at it in the next couple of days?"

"Yes, I'll do that. What are you looking at?"

"It's a riverside property–4511 Riverside. It's a couple of acres and it would be easy to put in a dock. It's just coming on the market, so keep it quiet."

"I'll head that way tomorrow then."

"Thanks, talk soon."

Elin listened to the conversation, then stared out her window. She had a few things to sort out before tomorrow. Just as she got into her pyjamas, her mobile phone chimed to let her know someone had sent her a text. She looked at the screen and saw that it was Justin, so she quickly sent him a message asking him how his day went. It would have been his first day on the job. He messaged back that it was interesting but he had a lot to learn. The other workers there were being helpful, and Daniel was making sure he got the proper training.

Elin smiled as she saw the bond between Justin and Daniel growing. She was thankful they got along so well. Justin asked about her day. She told him about getting the boat ready to go out tomorrow. She also mentioned that

Casey would be going out with her. It took Justin a few minutes to respond. Elin knew he was looking for the right words to say. Heck, even she didn't know what to make of it all. He wished her an abundant harvest, then told her he was exhausted and was going to lie down. She sent him a hug then turned off her phone.

Elin headed to the kitchen for coffee and dessert. Too much thinking could turn a good evening into a sad one. She didn't want to go there today. Fancy followed along beside her. Elin entered the kitchen to see a table full of dessert choices. She eyed the choices, then took a couple pieces as Roy and Heather filled their plates.

The coffee had just finished so they each poured a cup as they headed for the living room. Elin turned to the weather channel to see what tomorrow would bring. It looked like it would be cloudy. That would be good, as the cooler it was outside the more the fish would come upstream. They finished their desserts and then Elin excused herself to go to bed as she needed to be at her boat by 6 am tomorrow morning.

Roy and Heather cleaned up the dishes then put the extra desserts away before they made their way up to their rooms for the night. They both had things they wanted to take care of, and it was better to do it without any sort of interruption. Roy began looking at his finances. He also looked through some listings that the real estate agent had sent him. Then, he sent a text off to Andrew just asking how his day went, he wasn't sure he would answer back but it was worth a try. It took a little while, but Andrew answered.

When Heather went to her room, she sat down on the bed. She was feeling a little exhausted today. Then she realised that it had been a full month of dealing with one thing after another. She rolled into bed and closed her eyes.

After a time of tossing and turning, Elin padded down the hallway to the kitchen to grab herself a soda. Sleep was not coming easy tonight, even though she knew it was important that she get adequate sleep, as fishing was physically demanding. She sat at the kitchen table thinking about what the next few months would bring. There were good things and not so good things, but it would all come together. Finishing her soda, she put the glass in the sink, then headed back to her room.

Chapter Twelve

Elin woke up at 5 am. She made up a lunch, plus a couple of thermoses of coffee, taking along some scones for their morning break. Once she had it all together, she grabbed Fancy's leash, snapped it on her collar and headed for the vehicle. The sun was just starting to rise but there was a thick mist hovering over the town. She knew that in an hour or two it would burn off. It was looking like it may be a beautiful day. As she neared the car park, she saw that Casey was already there.

After everything was in the boat, Elin untied it as she started to head down the river to her favourite fishing spot. Her phone chimed a couple of times, but she was busy getting everything set for fishing, so she just ignored it. Once they arrived at her spot, they set the nets and floats, then sat down for their morning break. She took a quick glance at her phone. Heather had called but she was outside of mobile phone range now. Watching the sun come over the mountains was one of her favourite things to do. Her first day of the fishing season never struck her until the sun broke through the morning fog.

After their break, they moved the boat a little so that they could continue to fill their nets. Elin glanced at her phone again. There was a text from Justin asking her if she had felt the little earthquake that shook the capital. She found a slight signal and messaged him back that she didn't feel anything. He wrote back that it was only a 2.5 so it wasn't very big, but it felt like a wake-up call especially after the previous evening's tsunami alert for the west coast.

Casey was watching the waters. He motioned that the nets were getting full, so Elin ended her conversation and looked at the nets below. It was time to draw them in. They pulled them in, putting the fish into coolers. They both agreed that they should drop the nets again as it was still early enough in the day. Today looked like it would be an amazing fish haul, which made Elin begin to relax a little. Fancy curled up at Elin's feet as she opened the lunch bag and handed some food to Casey. He hadn't been very talkative this morning. Elin was almost afraid to bring it up as it was such a peaceful day.

After they had finished their lunch, Elin looked over at Casey and saw that he was deep in thought. For Casey, who liked to live life openly, that seemed a little odd. She touched his hand, at which point he looked over at her.

"How's it going, Casey? You've been pretty quiet this morning."

"Sorry about that. I didn't get much sleep last night."

"Of course, we all slept a little uneasily after the tsunami warning. Is anything else troubling you?"

"A few things that I need to work out. However, it does feel great to be out fishing with you again."

"It does feel good, doesn't it? Thank you for helping. I wasn't sure what to do after Justin headed South with Daniel."

They both stopped chatting as they started to watch the seals diving down for their dinner. Then the seagulls flew in to try to steal their fish. The story never changed but it never got old. There was a flock of ducks that was bathing near the shoreline.

A few boats started heading back to dock so Elin and Casey brought up their nets once more to put the fish in the coolers. It had been a good day fishing. Elin was sorting a cooler for Casey to take with him as well as one for her own use. The rest would be sold at the seafood market. That would help pay the bills for another month. Both of them were feeling the fatigue as they landed at the boat ramp, so Elin popped up to her vehicle to bring down the cart. They put the coolers on the cart, making a couple trips back and forth. Casey put his fish in his vehicle as Elin got ready to head to town to sell the other fish. He gave her a gentle hug as he got in his pickup truck.

Elin made it to the market in record time. She noticed that Andrew was working the car park. It seemed a little odd, but she really didn't know that much about Andrew. He let the other worker help her with her fish. Elin was smart enough to know, it wasn't a snub but an understanding that they were sort of related. Once the fish were weighed, the worker went inside for the cashier to write the cheque. Then, Elin was off to the bank before heading home to take care of the fish she had kept. She got another text from Justin. He told her that he missed Emma. Elin knew that would be an issue, but Justin seemed to be working through it. She sent him a hug and told him to call her tonight.

Emma was missing home, especially Justin, but she spent the morning getting settled in with her grandma. Then there was lunch with the two sisters before they went to see grandpa at the hospital. She was looking forward to seeing him and making sure that he was doing all right. The sisters told her he was doing fine but she needed to see for herself. Justin messaged her about a little earthquake that they felt earlier. They chatted about the tsunami warning from the night before. It was all old hat to Emma as it was with most people who lived on the west coast of the island, but it was great to hear from Justin. She was thinking of heading home a day early. She could take the long route back home through the capital.

Planning her time around the surgery was one of her ways of controlling the fear. So far, it had worked very well. She had to admit that she missed Scout and Ziggy as well as being home in their old family home, which looked like it was going to be permanent. Her other grandma was talking about selling their cottage in Allerton, now that both her and Jason were adults. She knew it was important for grandpa to stay where he was going to be able to stay on top of his heart issues. Her grandma made the comment gently. It took Emma back at first but then she had to acknowledge the years they had given to help her and Jason after their parents' passing.

Usually, Emma enjoyed the pace and the noise of the bigger cities on the mainland but this time she felt a little annoyed by it all. It was probably because of all the uncertainty over her grandpa's health. Then there was the need for Emma to prepare herself for surgery as well as her new schooling that was starting in the autumn. She had to admit it was much easier when she was a kid, and all the decisions were made for her. The school that she had chosen had already enrolled her. They had sent her the curriculum for the autumn sessions so she was going to do some shopping for some of things she would need for that. The two sisters were downright giddy to go shopping for her designer supplies.

Grandma's sister decided to shop in the hospital auxiliary store while they visited with grandpa. Going up in the elevator to see her grandpa, brought a flashback to when she was first admitted to children's hospital after the car incident. Even though hospitals weren't her favourite place to be, she knew how important they were to help you recover. As she neared her grandpa's room her grandma gave her hand a squeeze.

Emma peeked around the corner. Grandpa saw her and started to grin. It wasn't hard to relate to that feeling as each time they came to visit her in the hospital it gave her a small feeling of joy. She gave her grandpa a big hug. Then they pulled two chairs nearer his bed. They talked about almost everything until grandpa seemed to be getting a little tired. A nurse came in to take his vitals. Emma and her grandma gave him a kiss on the cheek as they left, telling him they would be back later.

Once downstairs, they decided to head to the mall. It would be a wondrous day of shopping and just being together. Emma found a lot of the items that she needed to have, to start school. The rest of the items she could order online once she got home.

Justin sent her a message, then the ladies realised that it was past dinner time. They stopped to pick up take out before heading home. Emma and Justin chatted while the two sisters sat up front, making their way through traffic until they reached their turn off. Once back at her grandma's house, Emma quickly went to the washroom and washed up. She was feeling a little homesick but was determined to spend a few more days on the mainland. Tomorrow, they were supposed to go visit some of her cousins who she hadn't seen in a very long time. It would be a bit of a drive but if they planned it well, they would miss the rush hour traffic.

She decided to call her other grandparents when she got to her room. She wasn't sure if it was homesickness or just needing to hear their voices. So much was changing, she was beginning to feel a little anxious. She spoke with them until her other grandma called her for dinner. It was a little noisy on the phone, so Emma asked them what it was. They told her that Scout wanted in, but the noise sounded different.

Austin went upstairs and saw that Raymond had completed a fair chunk today. Raymond wiped his hand across his face which took some of the sweat off, along with a lot of dust. It had been a busy day, but he was happy with the progress that he was making. Austin had been coming back and forth to help when needed. Raymond appreciated both his help and his company.

Casey would be helping him tomorrow. Today he had decided to help Elin as she was going out fishing. It was an odd change of events, but Raymond knew that Casey felt quite lonely since he and Elin went their separate ways. He understood that Elin had no choice as she worked to maintain her sobriety. Whatever came of today, Raymond hoped they both found a good place to relate to each other as they had been friends for a long time.

Tomorrow he and Casey would work on a manufacturing table where the sewing machines could be kept. He also wanted to start on an empty table space where fabric could be laid out and cut. He had to smile, he never thought he would be doing this kind of work. All the time spent learning carpentry was coming in handy. His focus was fishing but today he had handed that over to Melanie. She had found someone to help with the workload. Lately, he noticed that his mother had seemed a little happier. Her relationship with Melanie had grown and developed into something positive. They were all past the teen years, so maybe adulting was an eye opener for Melanie. He knew that until he hit adulthood it was easy to blame others for his circumstances.

There was a knock at the door, so Raymond looked up. He saw that Melanie was watching him.

"Hey, bro, it's dinner time. Mom sent me to remind you."

"It is. How did fishing go today?"

"It was really good. We got a large catch. I kept a cooler full for us before I sold the rest at the market. Do you want me to go out again tomorrow?"

"We can talk about that over dinner. I need to pack up a few things, then I will be right home."

"Anything I can help with?"

"Sure, could you unplug the tools while I pull the plywood into the room?"

"Consider it done."

When they were done, Raymond popped into the kitchen to wish Austin and Iris a good night. He told them that Casey would be helping tomorrow. They thanked him for a good day's work. Austin asked if there was anything he could do tonight to make it easier for them tomorrow. Raymond thanked him but told him everything was going as the plan. Austin let them out and then went back to the kitchen.

"Austin, do you think it's time that we moved back to our own home? That would leave the house for Jason and Emma."

"I've been wondering that, too. I don't rightly know just yet. Let's see how Emma's surgery goes, then we can make that decision."

"OK. Do you think we could do a day trip to our place one day this week? Raymond is okay to be alone in the house."

"Let's make that a plan," Austin grinned.

They finished their dinner. It felt odd without the kids, but they were able to relax a little. Iris went upstairs to get her needlework as Austin nodded off on the sofa. It had been so long since they had a quiet night.

The phone rang. It woke Austin so he headed for the phone as Iris put her needlework down. From the sounds of the conversation, it must have been Jason checking in. He did that every night. After chatting for a while, Austin handed the phone to Iris. She asked Jason about his day then Jason asked about the studio room. Iris told him it was coming along well, both Casey and Raymond would be there tomorrow. That seemed to please Jason. They all said good night as Iris hung up the phone.

Iris went to the kitchen to make their nightly tea. She noticed that the sun had just set. The sky was magnificent. She gave a quick thank you for the day they had just finished. Austin came into the kitchen as Iris put the cups on the table. He gave her a little hug, then sat down to fix his tea. After tea, Iris cleaned up the dishes then headed upstairs to get ready for bed. Austin wasn't ready to go to sleep yet, so he turned on the TV to look for something to watch.

Justin sat in his room and wondered if he was going to be able to do the job that Daniel had set up for him. It wasn't as easy as it had sounded. For Justin, it was his first foray into the financial world. He knew Daniel was giving him a lot of leeway to learn the job, but he hoped he wasn't disappointing him. His phone dinged. Emma had sent him a message. Apparently, she would be coming home a day early as she wanted to make sure she was all set up for her surgery next week. She was going to do the route to the capital, then bus up island to where Jason went to school. Jason would drive her back to Allerton.

She asked if they could meet for a lunch, or a dinner. Justin began to think about how to make that happen. He went downstairs and asked Daniel if he would be able to take a couple of hours off when Emma came through town. Daniel smiled as he told him that he would set it up for him. Justin quickly sent a message to Emma telling her that it would work for him.

While he was sitting back in his room, Justin decided to call the centre where his mother was staying. The nurse told him that there was no news at this point, which was a blessing. Justin asked her to let his mother know that he called and was thinking about her. He was told that she would do that as soon as they hung up. He felt it was important that he and his mother were connected some way, for now this was it. While he didn't understand why she stayed with his father, he believed that she thought it was better for the kids to have both parents. There were some good times. He decided he would hang onto those and let the rest go.

As it was the middle of the month, the company had given him an advance on his monthly salary. It was considerably more than he had made when he helped his father build fences, but he knew that he needed to be frugal as the job was only until the end of the summer. If he was smart, maybe he could rent a nice place in Allerton for him and his mother, although previous attempts to live together didn't work out too well. Well, today was enough for today. Justin grabbed his robe as he headed to the washroom for a shower. Everyone at work seemed to be a poster for hygiene so he was determined to fit in. He made sure his fingernails were clean, his hair washed, and that he used an extra dose of deodorant in the morning. He had to look hard into the mirror to recognise the person reflected there.

As he reached his room, he heard his phone ringing. He quickly made it to his desk. It was Elin.

"Hi, Elin," Justin answered.

"Hey, Justin. How's it going in the big city?"

"Pretty good. Trying hard to learn all the different jobs they want me to do. I hope that I'm doing well enough to warrant all the times that Daniel spends training me."

"From what Daniel told me, you are doing well. Just keep on doing what you're doing."

"It's different than anything I've done before. I'm not sure where all this is leading, but I'm willing to give it my best."

"That's what I wanted to hear. Know that Daniel and I both care a great deal about you."

"Thanks, Elin. Sometimes, I get caught in the past and have to pull myself out of the pit. Tonight, was one of those times, then you called. Thank you, Elin."

"Not a problem. You know the phone works both ways. If you need someone to talk with, I am here."

"I will keep that in mind. How was fishing this week?"

"It was great. Good hauls both days I went out. Casey came with me once, then Melanie came with me the other time."

"Melanie? Really?"

"We make a wonderful team. She's knowledgeable about fishing, plus we had some time for girl talk."

"Glad it worked out. Do I still have my job when I come back to Allerton?"

"If you still want it, of course."

"That's good to know. I really do like fishing."

"See, it runs in the family. Well, I'll let you go now. Have a good sleep and keep in touch, please."

"Will do, Elin. Good night."

Justin hung up the phone as he got ready for bed. It was early, but he was exhausted. Just as he finished dressing there was a knock at his bedroom door. He opened it up and saw Daniel grinning from ear to ear. He invited Justin downstairs for a cup of tea. When they got downstairs, Daniel's wife and daughters were already seated. It was a time to just talk about their day, to hear what the other members of the family were doing.

Daniel's daughters were still in university so there was a lot of talk about that. Daniel's wife, Irene, spoke briefly about the daily challenges of being an ER doctor. When it was Justin's turn, he just gave thanks for being a part of their family for the summer and how exhausting it was to change careers. They all nodded as change of any kind takes a lot of energy. Daniel talked about the upcoming summer challenges as staff took holidays. By then, Justin would be ready to carry some of that load. When they finished their tea, everyone went their own separate ways.

Emma was starting to plan her trip back to the island. She and Justin would have lunch on her way back. Then she'd hop the bus up island to where Jason lived. The homesickness seemed to be getting a little intense, she was even missing Scout. Grandma Ravinser told her that they had put the Allerton property on the market. Even though it made Emma a little sad, she understood. She got ready for bed, then spent a little while looking over the curriculum that the school had sent her. It looked very interesting. She was glad she had made the right decisions about school. Emma heard a knock at the front door so she headed down the hallway to see who it might be, especially at this late hour.

She looked out the window in the door but didn't recognise who was standing there so she waited until her grandma had made her way to the door. When her grandma looked out the window she stood back quickly. Emma wondered who it was on the doorstep. Her grandma shook her head and they headed away from the door. Emma followed her into the kitchen.

"Who is that grandma?"

"Someone who shouldn't be here," grandma answered.

"Do you know them?"

"Yes, Emma, I know them all too well."

"Should I let them in?"

"I don't think so. That is your uncle, Adam. We have a cease-and-desist order in place. I just have to figure out whether to call the police or not."

Emma made a cup of tea for them. She tried to figure out what her uncle had done that would make it necessary for her grandparents to go to such extremes. The knocking on the front door stopped but, in a few minutes, there was knocking at the back door. Her grandma was getting more and more rattled. Emma knew it was important to find a solution, soon.

"Do you want me to call the police, Grandma?"

"Not yet. I'll talk with him through the door to find out what he wants."

Her grandma went to the back door. Emma could hear voices but couldn't make out the words. She waited with her phone ready in her hand. The voices got louder and angrier until Emma knew things were going in the wrong direction. She made the choice to call the police hoping that her grandma would understand. Ten minutes later, a police car pulled into their driveway. She could hear loud voices again. Emma headed to the back door to let her grandma know about the police, but her grandma had already opened the door. One of the police officers were putting her uncle in handcuffs as they asked her grandma if she was okay.

"I'm fine, officer. He wants to see his father, but his father is in the hospital. The hospital won't let him visit."

"Understood," the officer replied. "Do you want us to give him a night to think it over?"

"If he settles down, no. If he can't settle down, yes."

"Why are you doing this?" Adam yelled.

"You know why, Adam. Calm down or you'll be spending a night in jail."

"Just tell me why I can't visit my father?"

"You know why. Your temper gets the better of you, then you do stupid things. Are you going to settle down or are you going to jail?"

"You can't rule my life, not now, not ever!"

"Officer, please remove him from our property. If he settles down let him go. If not, do what you need to do."

The officers took Adam towards their patrol car as her grandma closed the door and locked it. She turned around to see Emma staring at her. She wondered how long Emma had been there.

"I guess you have some questions," her grandma started.

"Some, but it's not my business. I will gladly listen if I can help in any way."

"Oh, dear, you're so sweet. Maybe we can talk about it in the morning. We both have an early start tomorrow."

"Right. Out to visit some more of my family. See you in the morning, Grandma."

"Good night, my dear."

Chapter Thirteen

Andrew finished with the last of the day's seafood, then headed to the staff showers before heading home. He was grateful to have this job this summer. He was determined to understand the seafood industry from the bottom up. Looking outside he saw that it was already dark. He knew that he wasn't going to get to the bus stop to catch the last transit home. Just as he finished dressing, one of the managers came in to tell him there was a breakdown in one of the freezers. He asked Andrew to stay to help. Andrew decided it would be a good chance to learn more about the cooling systems, so he put on a clean apron and headed to the freezer section.

They worked hard and were able to take the frozen goods from the broken-down freezer to one of the freezers downstairs. Then the manager put in a call for a technician to come in the morning. Either the repair company would need to fix it, or they would need to purchase a new one. It gave Andrew a good look at what managing money and inventory came down to, the very basics that he so wanted to learn. Andrew realised his bus was long gone. That didn't worry him much as he would just sleep at the cottage where he had stayed before. It was easy enough to work around its security system. Besides, all he wanted at this point was to sleep. He walked the 20-minute walk to the cottage, then went to the attic room. He was surprised that his blankets and pillow were still there.

As he was falling asleep, he remembered that he needed to let his mother know what was going on, so he grabbed his phone to give her a call. She answered the phone on the first ring. Andrew could tell she had been waiting for him to come home. He apologised for not calling her earlier and told her he would give her a call in the morning. With that he said his good night, put down his phone then froze. It sounded like footsteps downstairs, so he stayed quiet. There was banging of cupboard doors, then he heard the front door open and close. He quietly went downstairs to lock the front door. Then he noticed the mess in the kitchen. Whoever had been in the cottage had searched through all the cupboards, leaving their contents on the floor. There wasn't anything Andrew could do at this point, so he decided to do the clean-up in the morning. He climbed the stairs back to the attic room, wanting only to sleep.

His phone alarm went off at 7:30 am. Andrew opened his eyes to see the sun rising above the fog. He was extremely hungry as he had forgotten to get himself dinner before coming to the cottage last night. He went down the stairs as his phone rang, it was his mother. They chatted for a few minutes then he got busy cleaning up the kitchen. He found some cereal still in the cupboard; plus, there was still some yoghurt in the fridge. But he desperately needed a coffee. After going upstairs for his rucksack, he headed into town to find a coffee shop.

A car drove into the driveway just after Andrew made it out to the motorway. A fellow got out of the car, checked that it was 4511 Riverside Drive, then installed a 'for sale' sign. He went to the door where he put on a special locking device that would allow access to real estate agents. After affixing the lock, the agent went into the house to look around. It looked very clean, so he went back out to his car and drove away. After he left, the bathroom door opened, Adam poked his head out.

After getting freed by the police yesterday evening, he made his way over to the island, heading for the cottage. It was just as he remembered it. He took time to go through each of the rooms. It still didn't explain who the young fellow that came downstairs this morning was, but he had cleaned up the mess so that worked for Adam. He looked out at the lawn where he saw the real estate sign. He knew that he couldn't stay here as people would be coming and going as they checked out the cottage. He got his things together before heading for the motorway.

Andrew made it to the coffee shop just as it was opening. He felt a little awkward but all he wanted was breakfast. As he sat down, he noticed that Elin was in the coffee shop as well. He wasn't sure she would want his company, so he got his own booth. The waiter came over to take his order. He ordered coffee and a cinnamon bun. When the waiter left, Elin came by his booth, taking a seat on the other side of the table.

"So, Andrew, you are up early. What's up?"

"Just need to have a coffee or two before work. I'm working at the seafood plant right now, trying to learn some new skills."

"I know, I saw you there the other day. Does Roy and Heather know that you are here?"

"I don't think so. You can let them know if you want. It wasn't made to be a secret, but things happened quickly. I started working at the beginning of this last week."

"Are you travelling between your home and here each day?"

"That was the plan, but after shift last night they asked me to stay so I just found a place to sleep in town."

"Where was that?"

Andrew shifted in his seat, then he looked over at Elin and smiled.

"I stayed at the cottage that belongs to Jason's grandparents. It was all I could find in a pinch."

"Well, that works but I have another option for you if you want."

"What's that?"

"Well, I have a house with a lot of bedrooms that aren't filled this summer. If you need a place, with a good breakfast including coffee, you are welcome to stay with me. That is, if you're okay with dogs."

Andrew just stared across the table at her trying to figure out if she had another reason for making the offer. Nothing in her manner suggested that, so he looked down at his coffee for a moment.

"That's truly kind of you. I like the cottage, but someone ransacked it last night. I cleaned it up this morning but whoever did that may return."

"Is it okay if I let Jason know about that?"

"Sure. I guess he's the caretaker while the grandparents are on the mainland."

"I believe so. Hold on while I give him a call."

Elin put in Jason's number then waited for him to answer.

"Jason. It's Elin. Sorry for calling so early but I'm having coffee with Andrew. He discovered that your grandparent's cottage has been ransacked. He cleaned it up, but I thought I should let you know."

"Elin. What time is it?"

"About 8:30 am. Did I wake you up?"

"Yah. Had a late-night working on some course work. Emma told me yesterday that the grandparents are putting the cottage up for sale as grandpa needs medical care on the mainland. Besides that, Emma and I have reached adulthood."

"Oh. That's a surprise. Can I let Roy and Heather know that it is going up for sale?"

"Sure. Are they looking to buy?"

"I believe so. Anyway, I am trying to convince Andrew to stay at my place when he works late at the seafood plant. Can you tell him how great it is to stay with me?"

"Sure, put him on." Elin handed her phone to Andrew.

"Hi, Jason."

"Andrew, if you need somewhere to crash, stay at Elin's, it's the best. Plus, she's a great cook. Give it a try, you won't regret it."

"OK. Will do," Andrew answered as he handed the phone back to Elin. Elin finished her conversation with Jason, then turned to Andrew.

"Andrew, please stay with me when you get stuck in Allerton. Here is my phone number and address. You heard the bit about Roy looking for property in Allerton. He really does want to get to know you."

"That would be an interesting change in my life, but I am up for that. Anyway, I need to get to work. Thanks for joining me for breakfast."

Andrew paid for his breakfast, and Elin's too. He left feeling much better than when he got there. He knew part of it was the coffee and part of it was the company.

Jason completed his call with Elin then pushed himself to get out of bed. He wasn't sure he would go to Allerton today as he would be driving Emma there in a couple days. He called his grandparents to ask them to take a drive by the cottage but when they answered they told him they were at their place up island. They promised him that they would check it out when they got back to Allerton tonight. He asked them how Raymond was doing with the studio. They told him that it was nearing completion. Raymond and Casey had been putting in many hours to get it finished before Emma got back. Jason told them he would spend a couple nights in Allerton when he drove Emma home, then he could drive her to the hospital for her surgery. He mentioned that Rosa wanted to be there for Emma as well. They told him she was more than welcome to spend a day or so with them. Jason thanked them for that, then told them he needed to go get his day started.

He walked into his kitchen and started the coffeemaker. It was important for him to be at the school in a little over half an hour as they were reviewing for the final exams. The exams would be fine. He knew that if he completed his remaining assignments he could be completely finished within a month. Rosa and he had still not sat down to have the talk about when he finished his courses. He knew they were both avoiding it. Life would need to change if Rosa felt the need to head to a bigger city. He had all but decided that he wanted to work from Allerton, he could commute to the larger centres as needed.

Once Casey and Raymond finished Emma's studio, he was planning to take his dad's office. He could turn it into his office with all the tools that he would need to work from there. However, that didn't take into consideration that Rosa would need a space to work on her designs. Jason let out a sigh as he sat eating his breakfast.

Jason noticed that Daniel had left him a message. That was odd as he and Daniel didn't usually message each other, although Jason had a great deal of respect for the Gray family. Apparently, he wanted to have a chat about a possible business proposition, which perked up Jason. What could Daniel's business have in common with his new career? Anyway, Daniel asked for a conference call at 4 pm today. Jason looked at his schedule, it was do-able, so he agreed to the call. Jason pulled into the university car park with just minutes to spare so he jogged to class. He sat down just as the professor started going through the pre-exam review.

Jason tried to focus on the course material but so many things were running through his mind. He emptied his mind of all the personal things that were co-existing in it and forced himself to focus. He hadn't made it this far to fail now. Taking notes helped so he grabbed his binder.

As they hit the road to go and meet with the family, Emma decided to text Jason about the incident with Adam. Emma was looking forward to meeting all the family but her overriding thoughts were of going home tomorrow. Her plans for stopping to see Justin were made; plus, she was looking forward to just being home. She wondered if the other set of grandparents would be bowing out gracefully as well. A part of her hoped they would just stay. It was selfish but the thought of not having them close by made her feel sad. If they decided to move back to their place it would only be 45 minutes away but that was still away.

During her time with her cousins, Emma made sure to take tons of pictures to share with Jason when she got back home. Her grandma and her sister were having a wonderful day. Emma wondered how grandma felt about the incident with Adam last night. They hadn't spoken of it this morning. She wondered how safe grandma would be when she left tomorrow, that made her leaving feel much more difficult.

The two sisters came to sit down next to her. They had noticed that she was a bit shy. Her grandma knew that their moving back to the mainland would cause Emma a little uncertainty. However, Emma had grown up so much over the last year that her grandma wasn't sure that the change in residence was what bothering her. As the day ended, the three of them said their goodbyes then headed for their vehicle. It really had been an enjoyable family day. When Emma got into the car, she let herself relax. She could feel her eyes wanting to shut. The two older ladies upfront were continuing their family stories. Emma smiled as she thought of all the things they had gone through together.

The car stopped and Emma opened her eyes. She couldn't believe it, but they were back at her grandmother's house already. The two ladies upfront gave her a bit of teasing about sleeping the whole way home, but Emma was feeling a little more rested than when she had started the day. Grandma's sister got in her vehicle to head home as Emma and her grandma went inside. The sunset was sinking in the sky so the two of them decided to get into pyjamas and meet back in the living room.

Emma was still in the hallway when she heard her grandma play the messages on the answering machine. There was one from Adam. From the sound of it, he had found himself a load of trouble. Emma continued along the hallway to her room to put on her pyjamas as she tried to think of how she could help her grandma with Adam's situation. She washed up before heading back to the kitchen. By that time, her grandma was already in her housecoat making some hot chocolate. Emma thought she should just let Adam's call go but a part of her knew she needed to know her grandma would be all right before she went back to the island.

"Hey, Grams, I heard Adam's call. Is there anything I can do to help?"

"I don't know just yet, Emma. Do you know any of the police in Allerton?"

"A couple. Constable Allen was the one who dealt with the situation when Jason and I were younger. He is kind but tough at the same time."

"Would you mind calling him to let him know that Adam is in Allerton?"

"I'll call the station and see who's on. If Constable Allen isn't there, I know a couple other officers that we have gotten to know over the years."

Emma called the station. It rang several times before someone picked it up.

"Constable Allen, here. How can I help you?"

"Good to hear you, Constable. This is Emma Ryan. I am calling for my grandma. Uncle Adam, her son, is currently in Allerton. He has some deep anger issues. She just wants to give you a heads up. There was an incident here last evening but, apparently, he headed for the island as soon as he was released. He may try to gain access to her cottage by the river so could you please keep an eye out for him?"

"Emma, long time since we talked. Do you have a picture of him. That would make looking for him a lot easier?"

"Do you have a number I could send one to?"

"Sure 819-604-2914. I will distribute the picture so we can keep an eye out for him. What is his last name?"

"His name is Adam Ravinser. He is about six-feet tall, brown hair, blue eyes. He seems to be struggling with some mental health issues."

"OK, Emma. Send through the picture. We'll keep an eye out for him. Can I reach you at this number?"

"Yes. I am here until tomorrow morning. Grandma's number is 520-918-4421."

"Okay. Thanks for the heads up. We'll let you know if he turns up here."

"Thanks, Constable."

Emma hung up her phone and turned to her grandma. She was not sure she should leave her with Adam on the loose. It must have showed on her face because her grandma smiled at her. She thanked her for calling the police in Allerton, then told her not to worry. Her sister had already decided to stay with her until her husband was out of the hospital. Emma smiled back at her as they headed in to watch the TV.

"Love you, Grandma. I want to be here if you need me, no matter what I am doing."

"Thank you, dear, but I will be fine. How about a quick morning visit with grandpa before you leave tomorrow morning?"

"I'd love that."

They finished their tea, deciding to make it an early night. Emma texted Jason to make sure he got her earlier text about Adam, just in case. She also sent a text message to her other grandparents as well as Justin. She was more tired than she realised. Within a few minutes she was asleep.

The sun was streaming through the bedroom window and her phone was ringing when Emma opened her eyes. She looked at the number on the phone. Seeing it was Jason, she turned over and answered it.

"Hey, Emma. Hope I didn't wake you up."

"You did, but it's time to be up anyways. We are going to visit grandpa this morning before I head home."

"Are you still stopping for lunch with Justin?"

"Yes. It will be a little bit later lunch, but he checked with Daniel and it's fine."

"Then you'll be here at about five, correct?"

"That's the plan. I so want to get home to Ziggy and Scout."

"I've decided to take a couple days off so I will be with you when you check into the hospital in a couple of days."

"Oh. Thanks. Are you sure you can do that at this time of year?"

"Yup. Got it all approved yesterday. I got some exciting news to share with you later. Better get my butt to class. Love you."

"OK, Jason. See you later."

Emma hung up the phone as she got up. She was looking forward to seeing grandpa, then heading home. It had been an enjoyable time away, but she needed to be back home. She could hear grandma in the kitchen making coffee. It took a few minutes to pack up her things, then she looked out of the window as she realised how deeply she loved her island home.

Taking her bags to the foyer, she heard her grandma singing the song she used to sing to her when she was in the hospital here. When she got to the kitchen, she gave her grandma a big hug. Grandma turned around to give her one back. They ate their breakfast, then grandma headed off to get ready for their day. Within half an hour, they were on their way to the hospital.

The visit with grandpa went well. Soon they were on their way to the ferry terminal. Traffic was always heavy at this time of day, so it was a slow crawl, but they finally made it to the departures gate. Emma got her bags from the boot. They said their goodbyes then Emma headed into the ferry terminal. It was a beautiful day to be on the water as the sun shone down and the air was sweetly fresh.

She found a seat near the window, so she sat there watching the city fade into the background. The visit had been good, but Emma was tired. She decided to snooze while she waited for the ship to reach the island.

The boat shifted a bit as it made a bit of a bumping sound. Emma woke up. She realised they were at her destination, so she messaged Justin that she was in his fair city. He said he was waiting in the terminal. She wondered how he had gotten there but decided to let it go, she would know soon enough.

Justin waved to her as she came off the ferry. Then he came to carry her bags for her. She noticed that Daniel was standing back. She wondered if he would be joining them for lunch. He waved at her, then left the terminal building. They decided to have their lunch down near the water. The restaurant was not as full as lunch time had passed. Emma decided to have a light lunch as she still had some travelling to do today. They chatted about Justin's job and all the things that were happening. It was a good time together, but all too soon it was time for Emma to catch her bus.

Emma went to buy her ticket while Justin made sure her bag was on the bus. Then they gave each other a hug. Emma got on the bus, found a seat, and settled in for the ride. Justin waved as he headed to where Daniel was waiting. She hadn't ever seen Justin so happy. She realised having this new job and living with Daniel's family was a big part of it.

Before she knew it, the bus was pulling into the bus depot. She could see Jason and Rosa waiting for her. She gave each of them a high five as she left the bus.

"Oh, Emma. It's so good to see you again."

"Good to see you, too, Rosa."

"Part one of the surprise is that Rosa and I will both be driving you home tonight."

"Awesome! Are you both staying a couple of days, too?"

"Yup. Cleared it with professors and grandparents."

Emma smiled; this was better than she could have hoped. She felt the need for her family right now. They had decided to eat once they got to Allerton, Emma was good with that. They mostly just chatted about all the things that were going on. She knew that Jason had a surprise. She could feel he was almost bursting but she would wait until he was ready to tell her. Maybe he and Rosa were getting married or maybe it was something else. The drive home seemed so short but there wasn't a quiet moment during the drive. They pulled into their favourite restaurant where they ordered the dinner special. It got quieter as they ate their dinner. Emma messaged both sets of grandparents as well as Justin to let them know that she was home.

When they arrived at the house the grandparents had it all lit up. Emma felt herself relax a little. She could hear Scout barking as they climbed the stairs. When she opened the door, he jumped up on her. Ziggy was meowing away. He finally let Jason pick him up. The grandparents stood back, watching the scene unfold. It was good to have them both home again.

Chapter Fourteen

Emma woke up to her bed shaking. Scout was whimpering on the bed. She looked around to see if she was just dreaming, then she heard the sirens going off around town. She heard some things breaking. Surely no one would be blasting at two in the morning. There was a knock at her door, then Rosa poked her head into Emma's room.

"What's happening, Emma?" she asked.

"Not sure, Rosa. That was quite the shaking so maybe there was an earthquake somewhere on the island."

The grandparents' door opened. They came out into the hallway, followed by Jason. Their mobile phones started to send out an alarm signal, so Emma picked up her phone to look at the information that was coming through. When she looked up, they could see the fear in her eyes, so they all went into her bedroom. The power flickered off. Jason turned his phone into a light. They decided it would be better to head downstairs to decide what to do next. Jason found Ziggy hiding behind his nightstand, so he gently picked him up, to carry him downstairs.

As he walked partly down the hallway he stepped on some glass and gave out a bit of a yelp. Emma and Rosa came running. Rosa took Ziggy as they headed downstairs while Emma went into the bathroom to gather some bandages and hydrogen peroxide. She led Jason into the washroom, removed the shard of glass from his foot, then poured on the peroxide before putting on a bandage. It bled through rather quickly, so she added a few more bandages until the bleeding stopped. She helped him over to the stair lift. He rode down on the seat while she walked beside him. The others had gathered in the living room as grandpa was getting their battery-powered radio to work. The power flickered on and off a few times. They got some candles lit, then sat together. Emma and Jason worked away on their phones to find more information about what was happening.

"Well, what I could find out was, there was a large earthquake just north of the island. There has been some damage. They are expecting after-shocks, then possibly a tsunami," Jason reported.

"What do we need to do, Jason?" Rosa asked.

"For right now, just sit still. There has been some damage locally. In fact, some of the city centre structures are very damaged."

There was another shaking. This time Emma moved closer to her grandma and hugged her. Grandpa held Scout on his knee as he whimpered. Ziggy hid behind Jason and Rosa. They all held their breath until the shaking stopped. There was a grating noise. They wondered when it would all stop. Some more pictures fell off the walls as the dishes in the kitchen cupboards rattled. When the rattling stopped, Emma went to the back porch to find their old camping kettle. She picked up some newspaper and kindling just outside the back door. Jason got to his feet as she came back. He put the paper and kindling in the fireplace then got some matches from the desk drawer. Soon the fire was going well. Jason went to the back room for the grate so they could put the kettle over the fire in the fireplace as Iris hunted through the kitchen to find some snacks.

The early warning sirens continued to blare. They waited to hear if there was any tsunami alert, but so far, the news didn't carry that information. Jason went upstairs to get his slippers making sure to avoid the glass on the carpet. Austin went outside the front door where he looked around the neighbourhood to see what was happening. Everything seemed quiet for now. A few houses had candles glowing in them while others were still dark. He wondered if he should go over to Raymond's house to invite them over. He decided it might come easier from Jason, so he asked Jason to contact Raymond to see if they wanted to come over for a cup of tea.

The news they all hoped wouldn't come, came rolling out of the radio. The Emergency Preparedness Service messaged that a wave had been detected in the Northern Pacific Ocean. It was due to hit the island in about 45 minutes. They all looked at each other wondering what to do next. Where they lived, they were high enough that the wave would not reach them but all the people near the river were being told to move to higher ground.

Jason called Elin to see if she was okay or if she would like to make her way to their place. She told him that she and Andrew were going to bring her boat to higher ground before the wave hit. Jason offered to help. She asked him to meet them at the boat ramp in five minutes. Jason ran upstairs to put on work clothes. He was in his vehicle and at the boat ramp as she drove in. She backed the vehicle with the boat trailer down the boat ramp. Andrew and Jason jumped out to guide the trailer under the boat. Once it was in place with the security rails up, they were off to Elin's place. When the boat was in place, Jason headed back home.

At the cottage, Adam was awakened from his sleep. No one had thought to fasten the firewood door, so he had carefully made his way through it just after dark. Now, the whole cottage was shaking. Things were smashing on the floor. He sat there with his hands against his ears rocking back and forth. The shaking stopped so he got to his feet to head downstairs. There was a lot of broken glass, so he manoeuvred down the stairs carefully. When he got to the main floor he sat down, looking around at his surroundings.

Just as he started to get to his feet, there was another grating sound then more shaking started. He sat down again, waiting for it to end. As he crawled towards the living room, he hoped that he could find shelter there. Pictures had fallen off the walls and the TV had fallen from its perch. He needed to stay calm, to think clearly, but the chaos was starting to get to him.

He picked up his phone to dial his mother's number, then quickly turned off the phone. There was no point adding more stress to an already dicey situation. He heard the sirens outside and wondered what they were all about. It had been two decades since he had spent any time on the island. Wanting to know more about the sirens, Adam turned on his phone as he began to search for any information he could find about the sirens. His search took him to the emergency programme website. He gasped when he read that the sirens meant a tsunami was building. It said that it would hit the inlet in the next half hour or so.

There were a couple of local places where people could head to so that they were out of the path of the tsunami, but Adam wasn't sure where they were. He decided he could follow some of the vehicles that seemed to be heading for higher ground. He also considered getting in touch with Emma or Jason. However, he thought they may be reluctant to help him after what happened at his mother's place. The directions to the reception centre were on the city's website so he went to his map programme as he headed outside.

Just as Adam got to the motorway, there was another tremor. He stood still and hoped it would stop soon. He had seen movies where the road opened up, where people and cars had fallen in the opening. He prayed he would make it safely to the reception centre. As he was getting closer to the centre, he saw a car park full of vehicles. People were hanging around outside the building. Inside there was a calmness. Adam thankfully took a coffee and found a place to sit. To register, he would need to stand in a queue. At this moment he wasn't sure he could do that.

His head ached and he felt disoriented. One of the people giving out blankets came over to him as they noticed that he was struggling. They spoke to him briefly then went to get a medical person to help him. Adam tried to stay calm, to think things through. It was tough but he knew it was vital or they would either hospitalise him or put him in police custody. He wasn't willing to do either.

A police officer came over to him and asked him his name. Adam just looked at him trying to decide if he should tell him or not. The officer glanced at a piece of paper in his hand, then showed it to Adam. There was no denying that it was a picture of him. He tried to stand up, but he felt a little faint, then all he saw was darkness. The police officer grabbed him before he hit the floor. Someone brought a stretcher to put him on. They took him over to the medic room where the doctor looked at him.

"Who's this?" the doctor asked.

"I believe it's Adam Ravinser. I got a call earlier to be on the lookout for him."

"Do you know what caused him to faint?"

"No, not really. I know he has anger issues and that he came here a day or so ago."

"That's not really helpful at this point. We'll see if we can revive him. We'll probably send him to the hospital for observation."

"Sounds good. Do you need my help?"

"Not at the moment, but if he resists going to the hospital, we may need you to bring him in under the mental health act."

"I'll be here for the next several hours so let me know if you need any help."

Constable Allen left Adam with the paramedics. He started going through the crowd, watching for anyone that was in distress. He gave out a couple of blankets and a few cups of coffee as he watched to see how many more could fit into the reception centre. He radioed the station to ask for another officer to help out, but they told him that they were all busy. The sound of the sirens was eerie in the darkness.

People were jittery and the loud noise just made it worse. He saw that someone had set up a childcare area. Several babies were sleeping in strollers while a few toddlers were cuddled up in sleeping bags on the floor. He was thankful it wasn't cold out tonight. Some of the parents took chairs, or sat on the floor, to be near their children while they rested. An ambulance pulled up, so the constable made his way over to the medic area. They were placing Adam in a stretcher-chair that would go on the ambulance. He was resisting a little, but they had it under control. When the officer approached Adam, he looked at him, then looked away.

After Adam was in the ambulance, the constable looked up the phone number Emma had given him for Adam's mother. He made a quick call. It rang four times before she answered.

"Mrs. Ravinser, we have found Adam. He is being taken to the hospital for observation. He came to the reception centre which was good as we're expecting the wave to hit soon."

"Thank you, Constable. Our prayers are with you and the people on the island. My granddaughter and grandson are there as well but I believe they are above the inundation zone."

"Are you talking about the Ryan family?"

"Yes."

"They are well above where the wave will hit but I will make sure to check in with them later."

"Thanks, Constable. Oops, we just got a little shaker here. I'd better see if my sister is okay."

"Okay. Stay safe."

The officer took another walk through the crowd. He saw that the emergency personnel were managing well through all the confusion. He poured himself a coffee and found somewhere to sit. His phone rang a warning, so he looked down. He saw that the wave had reached the inlet and was heading down the river. A voice came over his radio that people had started to gather at the river to see the wave come through. He just shook his head. All available units were told to head down to the shore to get people to move to higher ground. He looked around and saw that everything was peaceful. He went out to his police car to head down to the river. They had 15 minutes at the most to move the people back.

He looked over and saw that someone had brought their children to the river. He decided to start with them so he told them to go to higher ground or they would be arrested, and their children would be handed over to the Ministry. Many of them left after being told to go but he wondered if they actually went to higher ground. Within a few minutes the riverbank where he had parked was empty. He got in his vehicle to head further along the river, but it seemed like most people had moved back. Looking over at the cottages along the river he wondered what they would look like in the morning.

The radio told all officers to head to higher ground as the wave approached. The villages along the inlet were already reporting the wave as coming through and that it had caused a fair amount of flooding. So far, the people had all been able to reach the village recreation centres or a reception centre that was above the inundation level. The mills along the river had dismissed all their employees. A few had decided to stay to ride out the wave as well as to make sure the mills stayed secure.

As the ambulance reached the hospital, Adam decided that he did not want to stay so they had to put him in under a mental health order. Once the nurses put him in his room he settled down. They took him a glass of juice and some medication, then left him as other patients were buzzing for their help. Two of the people who were being wheeled in had been at home convalescing but had to leave their homes. Adam closed his eyes as he waited until the staff were busy. Then he opened his eyes as he began to plan how to get out of there.

There was an announcement over the intercom that all available staff should head to the ER. For Adam that was perfect timing. He waited until they left the ward, leaving only one nurse to cover. More patients were asking for help again, so Adam waited until the nurse went into one of their rooms, then he slipped out the outside exit, setting off an alarm.

He ran as quickly as he could in bare feet, making it to the forested area near the hospital before anyone came looking for him. He had grabbed his jacket on the way out, so he sat down on it trying to think of where he could go. The cottage was out as it was close to the river where the wave would hit. He could see the security guards checking the area looking for him. He got behind the trees, hoping they would move on. There was a dog barking. When he looked around, he saw an officer with a dog checking out the car park. Still staying as quiet as he could, he moved a little further into the forested area. Suddenly, he felt something knock him over. He covered his head trying to fight off whatever it was. Moments later there were people all around him. The officer called off the dog as another officer handcuffed Adam.

Adam's anger raged as he tried to get free from the officer's grip. He was swearing and crying at the same time. The officers sat him down on one of the benches near the car park. They let him compose himself, then gently walked him back into the hospital. The nurse gave him another sedative before they took him back to his room. Constable Allen got the 'all-clear' to head back to the reception centre but he took a couple minutes to visit with Adam. He let Adam know he would be back tomorrow. Hopefully they could find a way for him to return to the mainland.

The roads were mostly empty as Constable Allen reached the reception centre. A woman came up to him, pleading for him to help her find her son who had gone missing down near the river. The wave was already making landfall, so the officer asked her whereabouts they had been. He felt maybe he could make it there as it was not at sea level, but he knew that it would be unlikely he would find the child. The mother hopped in his vehicle as they headed to where she had last seen the child.

They could see the wave making landfall, with logs and other debris crashing together. As they neared the spot where the mother had last seen the child, the mother jumped out of the car. The officer looked along the path to see if there was any movement. With no streetlights it was nearly impossible to see but he thought he heard something a little way down the path. He parked his vehicle then grabbed his torch light as he started towards the sound. As he got closer, he saw a small child playing in the sand box, building castles. The child looked up as the officer came close. The officer bent down and picked him up. He called for the child's mother, but she didn't answer so he carried the child back to the vehicle.

He drove closer to where the mother had jumped out of the car. He could hear her calling for the child.

"He's with me!" the officer shouted.

"Where are you?" the mother asked.

"Pretty close to where you got out of the vehicle, just follow the headlights."

"I can't see the headlights."

"How about my torch light, do you see it?"

"No. Can you put on your hazard lights; they may help?"

"Done."

It got incredibly quiet, then the officer saw the woman start to climb the riverbank. The wave was just behind her, but so far, she was keeping ahead of it. She reached the pathway as the officer opened the door. It took all that the vehicle had to pull away from the water as it started to drift onto the path. He floored the petrol pedal, and they moved a little ahead of the water. He tried to get onto the road leading to the reception centre, but it wasn't possible, so he went the other way, ending up on Elk Drive.

Driving along, the officer noticed that the Ryan household had candles burning so he decided to see if they could take in the mother and child. He called the home phone, but it was not in service, so he sent a quick text message to Emma's phone. It took about five minutes until she messaged back telling him to bring them over. After the mother and child were comfortable at the Ryan's, the officer radioed into the station to ask where they would like him to go next. They told him to just stand by, so he accepted a cup of tea as he waited to hear where they wanted him to go.

One of the officers began giving a radio update of the tsunami. There had been a fair amount of damage, a lot of the boats at the marina were set adrift making it even more challenging. The warning sirens continued to blare out into the darkness. Everyone just sat and got quiet. The child was asleep in his mother's arms, so she leaned back in the recliner. Scout whimpered so Emma thought he may need to go outside. She took him out the back door to let him do whatever he had to do. He quickly came back to her, so she gently led him into the house. Everyone was very quiet. Emma decided to go to her room to see what she could find on the streaming news networks. There was some reporting from a couple of the small villages along the river but other than that there was nothing.

She messaged Justin but there was no response, so she figured that he was still asleep. It was about an hour before she received a text from Daniel. He told her that Justin was driving back to Allerton to find his mother who had gone missing from the centre. Emma went downstairs to let the family know what was going on with Justin.

"Jason, you said you had a surprise to share with me earlier. Can I ask you what that was?"

"That seems like a long while ago, even though it was just a few hours. There is a couple of things. One, Daniel's firm wants to open a satellite office somewhere on the central island. He wanted to know if I would want to rent some space to do my work in. Second, I got notified that I can write my exams next month to complete my studies."

"Wow, those are both great! Have you made any plans yet?" Emma commented.

"Not yet. It just all happened in the last day or so."

"Do you think there would be a place for me when I finish my studies?" Emma asked.

"That's possible. Would you want that?"

"Not sure. I'll need to think on that."

"So, Jason, are you going to stay on the island when you finish your studies? We know you've been debating that," his grandma asked.

"Gram, that will depend on a couple of things. I'm still thinking it over."

"Grandpa and I have been wondering if you move here, would it be a suitable time for us to move back home?"

"No, Gram!" Emma shouted. Everyone looked around at her, she was crying.

"Don't cry, Emma. We wouldn't be far."

Emma went over to sit near her grandma. It had been too much for one day. They all realised that Emma was still a little upset about the other grandparents moving back to the mainland. The conversation changed as Jason went upstairs for his laptop. He found a news station that was live streaming so they could see the tsunami from an outside view.

A change of subject brought the tension down and the officer decided he would try to make it back to the reception centre. He radioed in his change of venue as Iris got some biscuits for the officer to take with him. She told him they could take the mother and child to the reception centre in the morning.

Emma and Jason decided to get in the car to head over to Justin's parents' home. They thought they might see some clue that would suggest Justin's mother may have found her way there. Grandpa headed upstairs to get more blankets for grandma and the two sleeping on the recliner. Then he climbed the stairs, flopped on his bed, and drifted off to sleep.

Chapter Fifteen

Everything was so dark. There were so many sounds in the air. Adrianne covered her ears as she pushed the button. She waited for someone to come to help her as her legs were tangled up in her blankets, plus she needed to go to the washroom. Once again, she pushed the button but still no answer, so she tried to push the blankets off her. There was no way to get up, then her bladder let loose. She was wet and ashamed, so she covered herself back up so no one would see what she had done.

Putting her head back on the pillow she pulled the blankets up over her head, wishing she were dead. A nurse came in, looked around the room and thought that Adrianne had gone back to sleep. She went near the bed to look at her pillow, but Adrianne made no movement. The nurse went back out into the ward which was rapidly being filled with people who were caught up in the frenzy of the tsunami.

Adrianne took the blankets off one by one, then flipped her legs over the side of the bed. She would get up and change, even change her bedding as there was a fresh set of bedding on the counter. After pulling the wet bedding off she looked in the nightstand where she found her clothing, at least some underclothing. She undressed herself, putting on the items she had found. There was another nightgown on the counter as well, so she took it. Adrianne decided to take a walk into the hallway, then into the lounge. Everyone else was in their rooms. The one nurse on duty looked up and smiled as she saw Adrianne.

The power flickered off until the generator started. The night staff began to file back into the wards. They were at full occupancy so there was no more room to house anyone else. The staff began their debrief as Adrianne slipped out of the ward. The nurse looked around and saw that Adriane was not in the lounge anymore. She figured she had just gone back to her room. They would check to make sure she was all right as soon as she finished with the nightly statistics. In the meantime, Adrianne borrowed a jacket and some boots from the staff lounge. She was on her way to see her kids. She hadn't seen them in a very long time; besides, she needed to be sure they were okay.

Sheer instinct took her along the roads that led back to the house where she once lived. It didn't look like anyone was home, so she went in the back door noticing that her furniture had all been moved around. There was some food in the fridge and a coffee maker, so she tried to make coffee before realising that the power was off. Her husband must have forgotten to pay the bill or something like that. She sat in her recliner, rocking back and forth. It felt so good to be home, even without power.

Adrianne got up and went to the cabinet near the table, which was where she kept the candles. When she opened the drawer, she was surprised to see that nothing had changed. The candles and matches were right where she had left them. There were footsteps outside so she closed the drawer, bending down so no one could see her. She was going to see her kids before anyone took her back to that hospital.

Emma listened carefully at Justin's house. She thought she heard something in the house but there didn't appear to be any movement. Maybe it was mice or rats. Jason got out of the car, heading towards the house. Emma raised her hand for him to approach quietly.

They both stood outside the house and waited. After about ten minutes, Adrianne headed back to her chair with the candles and matches. Emma heard the movement, but they still waited to see who or what it was. Emma messaged Constable Allen to let him know that they were at the Knowles house and that someone may be inside. He messaged back that he was on his way. Emma sent a message to Justin to let him know where they were. He let her know that he was just approaching the town limits. Now, they just had to wait, which was one of the hardest things to do at a time like this.

Constable Allen pulled up, turning off his headlights and motor as he slid into the driveway. Emma went to his car to tell him about what they had put together so far. She also let him know that Justin was on his way. They all decided to stay put until Justin got there. They could still hear the tsunami crashing through town with the sirens still blaring. Hopefully everyone had made their way to higher ground by now. Within a few minutes, Justin pulled into the driveway. He looked tired and upset so Emma took his hand as he headed towards the house. He asked Emma to go inside with him. She looked at the officer who just nodded.

As they went up the steps, they heard someone moving about.

"Hey, Mom, it's me, Justin."

Everything went silent. Then they saw candlelight in the house. From what they could see it was indeed Adrianne.

"Mom, I'm coming in. Are you OK?"

There was still no response, so Justin went to the door and opened it. On the other side was his mother bathed in candlelight, smiling as big as he had ever seen her smile. Justin stepped forward as she gave him a hug.

"So glad you finally got home. Where is your brother? Is he down at the marina again?"

"I'm not sure, Mom, but it's nice to see you are safe."

"Why wouldn't I be safe? It's been a while since I've seen you but I'm always safe when you and Trevor are around."

"Mom, we rented out this house as no one was living here."

"Oh!"

Jason stepped into the house with Constable Allen. Adrianne took one look at Jason and hid behind the chair.

"Why did you bring him? He killed your father and your brother."

"Mom, that is Jason Jr. He was just a kid when all that happened."

"It was him. It was HIM!"

"Mom, it's okay. I'm here. I will make sure no one hurts you."

The radio the constable was wearing was reporting that the wave was starting to diminish in the downtown area. Adrianne looked at the constable, then over at Justin.

"Are you sending me to jail, Justin?"

"No, Mom, not now or ever."

"Tell him to get out of my house!" Adrianne said as she pointed at Jason. Jason took the cue, so he headed back outside. The story was old, but Adrianne still had not made peace with what had happened. Emma slipped out behind Jason. Tonight was one for the history books.

Justin walked his mother out of the house. He sat her down in Daniel's car as he explained to the officer that he would take her back to the centre. The officer moved aside. Justin told Emma he would stop in for a visit after his mother was settled. The officer took one more look around to make sure that no candles were left burning. Then he closed the door and locked it. As he got into his patrol car, he could see a few breaks of morning trying to make it through the darkness. He hoped that the daylight wouldn't show too much destruction.

He decided to drive to the Ryan household. Maybe he could bring the woman and her child back to the reception centre. When he got there, they were all dressed. Breakfast was being made on a camp stove on the back porch. He smiled at the scene as the woman collected her son, found their things, said a thank you to the Ryan's and headed out to his car. As the officer drove up to the reception centre, a man came running up to his car.

"Are you the constable who found my wife?"

"Possibly," he said as the woman poked her head out of the car. The man opened the door, grabbing the little boy as his mother got out of the car. The constable continued up the car park to the door of the reception centre.

Emergency personnel were making sure that those who had come to the evacuation centre were registered with Emergency Preparedness Allerton. Crews had started to assess the damage done to the city centre. There were properties that had suffered severe damage and would need to have major repairs. Then there were other properties that would only have a little water damage. Either way, as far as was known today, there were no fatalities. Several boats at the marina had been destroyed by the waves as well as the rocks and debris. Mainland cities were sending counsellors and first responders to help the residents as they headed back to their homes.

As Justin drove into the car park at the centre his mother began to get restless. She didn't want to go back inside, so she was trying to think of a way she could escape. Justin saw her reluctance to go back inside. He thought he would take her for a little drive, then they could chat a little.

"You know, Mom, I have a job in the capital. They are training me in the finance field. So far, they like the work I've been doing. They are thinking of opening an office in the central island region. That would mean I would work there, and we would have more time together."

"That would be nice," she replied. "Would we live together?"

"I'm not sure yet. We have a lot to figure out before then."

"What about Trevor? Would he live with us too?"

"You know what, Trevor will always be with us even if he won't be living with us. I loved him too, mom. He was so amazingly kind to me and you."

"He was," his mom answered as she began to cry. She leaned her head on Justin's shoulder as she fell fast asleep. Justin looked down at her, wondering how everything would work out. There was something else he should have told his mother. The firm where he worked was working on a fundraising campaign for the local Y, to sponsor programmes for youth. He knew that Emma would like that. Her father was setting up programmes with the Y director just before he died. That would be completion for many people.

Justin drove into the car park at the centre and gently helped his mother into one of their wheelchairs. The nurses came around his mom to hold her hand. Justin realised that they truly did care about her. The nurses wanted to talk to him after his mother was back in bed so after she was all tucked in, he made his way to the nurses' station. They apologised for her walking away from the centre. Justin listened, then told them she was safe now so that is all that mattered. He asked them how she was doing overall with staying there at the centre. They told him she was a model patient. However, once in a while she got a little nervous and wanted to go home.

He figured if he took the job on the central island, he could spend more time taking her out. As he walked back to his car, the doubts began to crowd in. He wondered what the next steps would be and if he was ready to take on the work that they wanted him to do. As he reached the Ryan house, he so wanted to talk with Emma. He hoped that there would be time for them to just chat, without the rest of the household around. If that didn't happen, then possibly he and Emma could go for a drive.

As Justin ascended the stairs, he saw Emma look out the window. Something so simple, made him feel so good. She opened the door, ushering him into the living room where she had set out food for him. He remembered then that it had been hours since he had eaten or slept. After devouring the delicious meal, he sat back in the chair and rested his head. Now would be the perfect time to talk with her. It was quiet, they were virtually alone. His eyes closed as he drifted off to sleep so Emma grabbed a blanket to cover him up. She messaged Daniel that Justin was taking a nap at their place. Daniel thanked her for letting him know and then told her to take care of Justin while he was there. Emma sat there watching him sleep. She could see the stress of the past few hours leave his face, he almost looked like a child sleeping. She decided to just let him be, so she went up to her room and started to work on her tablet.

Her grandma came up to her room to tell her they had found news reports regarding the tsunami. They were all going to watch it in the living room. Emma wondered if Justin would wake up, but she thought he was probably out for a while. She made her way downstairs and found a seat on the sofa as Scout padded over to her. He put his head on her knee. Ziggy wandered in as well, jumping up on Justin who stayed asleep without even moving. The news reports were graphic and scary. Emma wondered how the people of Allerton made out. There were not a lot of news stories about the island until they turned to an island news station. The pictures they shared were incredible. They were reporting a fair amount of damage but so far, no fatalities. Justin began to move around a bit as he slowly opened his eyes.

He saw Ziggy sound asleep on his lap while Emma was sitting on the sofa with her grandparents watching the local news. Justin wasn't sure how long he had been asleep, but he felt a little better. However, his body felt sore, so he wiggled around until he was sitting upright. Ziggy climbed up his chest and looked him straight in the eyes. There was no way he would get away from petting him, so he cuddled him a little and gave him a pet. It was time to start back to Daniel's house, but he just wanted to sit still for a little while longer, besides he and Emma needed to chat. She saw he was awake, so she went to get him a coffee. Justin was having a bit of trouble sitting up with Ziggy so close to his face, so Emma gently took him off Justin. She cuddled Ziggy as she took him over to the sofa.

After his coffee, Justin got up and went to the washroom to clean up a little. Jason walked by, telling him the shower was working if he wanted one. Justin just smiled. It was what he needed right now. When he came out of the shower, he saw that someone had taken his clothes and there was a fresh set. It was such a kind gesture that he almost wanted to cry. He found a disposable razor set out for him as well, so he did his daily routine, then headed downstairs. They were all still in the living room watching the news as it unfolded. It was getting close to lunch time. Justin remembered he had to fuel up before he left for the capital.

"Would you like to come for a short drive with me, Emma? I have to fill up the car before I head back to Daniel's."

"Sure, maybe we can take a peek around the river as well."

"That would be cool, if the roads are open."

Justin headed to the petrol station where he filled the tank. Then he looked for a road that would lead them to the river. They came across roadblocks at all the roads that entered the river properties, so they decided to get out to walk down to the river. As they passed the officers at the roadblock, they heard a radio call asking for help at Riverside 4511. Emma stopped in her tracks. She touched Justin's arm. He turned around and saw the fear on her face.

"What's up, Emma?"

"That property, it is my other grandparents' cottage. I need to find out what is happening."

Emma walked over to where the officers were standing. She asked about the radio call to the riverside property. They looked at her a little oddly, then shrugged their shoulders.

"The officer who is there is asking for assistance with something at that address. Do you want to go by and look?"

"Yes. I'll call my brother, he's the one who's in charge of the place right now. What kind of assistance is the officer asking for?"

"I'll ask the officer, just give me a minute while I go back to the car to find out."

Emma messaged Jason about the property. He was heading there right away. Justin was heading back to the car so they could go there as well. The officer came back and said that as far as he could find, the property received considerable damage. They were concerned about the propane tank that fuelled the appliances. Emma thanked him for his help as she headed back to the car. When she got there, they headed to the riverside property. Justin had messaged Daniel that he may be a little late getting back.

Daniel told him they still had a car so he could take whatever time he needed. That took the pressure off, at least a little. He still hadn't had a chance to talk with Emma. If this dragged on too long, he was afraid he would just shut down.

When they got to the roadblock near the cottage, Emma told them that the police officer near the marina told them about her grandparent's house. She told him that the officer told her to let the officers at the roadblock know that they had received permission to attend. Jason was already there. He came over as they were waiting at the roadblock. He and Emma had a short conversation, then they approached the cottage. The main floor had received a lot of water damage while the inside was damaged by falling pictures and shelf units. Emma went up the stairs to the loft to look around. Everything looked the same as it did before except for the blankets, pillow, and a sketch pad that was near the window. She went to her desk to pick up a few papers and put them in a folder. She had forgotten they were there; they would be helpful when she started classes.

Emma stopped to pick up the sketch book. The inside cover was filled with lots of different drawings that had been sketched, then erased, then sketched again. There was no signature anywhere, but a set of initials was found on the bottom of a couple of drawings. Emma couldn't think of anyone with the initials AW, so she scooped up the book, putting it with her things to take downstairs. As she started down the stairs, she felt the ground start to shake. She held onto the railing. It lasted less than a minutes but by then she was ready to run outside. She met Jason and Justin at the front door, as they headed outside.

The gas technician had arrived. They were told that they needed to vacate the property until he had shut off the appliances or anything else that would need propane to fire up. No one saw the man at the back of the cottage scoot off into the brush. He moved quickly towards the river. In the bushes, he watched to see if anyone had followed him. Now, he just needed to make it back to the boat on the other side of the island. Asher got on the path to the motorway, slowing down so as not to attract attention. As he watched the river, he noticed debris still floating along with the tide, there was even a pair of shoes–attached to a pair of legs. He stopped and stared at the scene before him but knew that he had to get out of there. He had no legitimate reason for being where he was.

Once the gas technician had shut off the gas, the police gave an 'all-clear'. Emma and Jason went back into the house. When they looked through the living room window all they could see was the 'for sale' sign. They remembered that the grandparents had just put it up for sale a day or so ago. Well, it would not be worth much in this shape. They would talk with their grandma after dinner tonight. Justin was getting a little restless, so he and Emma decided to finish their drive. They drove along the river road as far as they were allowed, then walked down to the riverbank.

"Emma, some things have come up over the last month or so. Daniel's firm is wanting to open a satellite office on the central island. They would like me to be part of that."

Emma stayed quiet, just listening, not sure what he was trying to tell her.

"It's a fantastic opportunity but it will come with a lot more responsibility. Some days, I wonder if I can do what they want me to do. Other days, I want to jump right in."

Emma remained quiet to give him a chance say what he needed to say.

"Emma, a lot depends on other things, like my mother, you and your family. Do you think your family would accept me if we dated seriously?"

Emma sat still for a moment, then smiled.

"Yes, Justin. They have come to respect you, especially after all that happened in the last day or so. None of us are the same as we were when things went down before my parents passed away. We miss them on the daily but know that we need to continue on, to make a way to honour what they gave us."

"Would you like to date on a more serious basis?"

"Wow. Do you really need to ask that? You are one of the constants in my life. While you are away this summer, I will miss you. However, it works out well as I'll be spending a good part of the summer in recovery from surgery. Do you think you will still want to date me without the scars on my face?"

They both looked out over the river, watching the sun dancing on the water. It felt like a fairy tale. The beauty of the moment was impeccable. Justin looked back at Emma and smiled.

"Scars or more scars, it doesn't matter. We have been friends so long that not having you around is lonely. I want to be here for you as you finish your surgeries. Daniel says I can take long weekends if I want. That will work well. I'm going to buy a newer car at the end of this month so then I can go back and forth whenever I want."

Emma bent over to give him a kiss as they headed back up to the car. The bank of the river was covered with branches, leaves, and other things that were swept into the water by the tsunami. Emma peered into the muddy water at the shore where she saw the small fish feeding on the insects near the bank. She missed the shoes, and the legs, that floated further out in the underbrush. When they got back to the car, they saw Jason had parked near their car. He honked at them, then headed off for home. He and Rosa had some thinking to do.

Chapter Sixteen

Justin drove up to Emma's house and gave her a hug. She hugged him, then got out of the car. She waved as he backed down the driveway, heading back to the capital. He was thinking ahead. For Justin that wasn't something he had done for some time. As he passed the mental health centre on his drive out of town, he remembered the way they had treated his mother. He wasn't anyone's fool; he knew she still had a lot of issues to deal with before she could function outside of the centre.

He was happy he had talked with Emma, things seemed to be progressing well. His one big concern was still the divide between the Ryan family and his mother because of the events that went down between the two. The alert on his phone beeped so he looked down to see what was coming in. There was another earthquake just north of the island. He waited to see whether they would issue a warning or just an alert, wondering if he should turn around or not.

Emma climbed out of the shower and grabbed her towel as the earth began to shake again. She wasn't necessarily afraid of the earthquakes, but they made everyone around her uneasy, including herself. Scout started to whimper as he waited outside the washroom door. Emma had to smile as he was never far from her when she was at home. Her grandma knocked on the bathroom door as Emma slipped into her housecoat.

"Emma, are you okay?"

"I'm good, Grandma. But I'm not sure Scout is."

"He's right here at the door, waiting for you. Come have tea in the kitchen if you want it."

"Thanks, Gram. I'll be down in a few."

She heard her grandma going down the stairs as Scout sprawled out on the other side of the washroom door. As she was drying her hair, she felt another little shake and began to wonder if something bigger was on its way. Turning off her hair dryer, she headed to her bedroom where she quickly changed her clothes then headed downstairs to the kitchen. It was good to see everyone seated around the table as she took her seat. They all looked a little more tired than usual so there was a lot less chatter. Ziggy felt left out so he jumped up on Jason's knee. Rosa looked at them and smiled. She and Jason had a good talk earlier. Things were beginning to work themselves out, little by little. They heard a car drive into the driveway, so grandpa got up to find out who it was. He opened the door to find Elin and Andrew there. They joined them around the table.

"Hello everyone! Jason, I brought you something to thank you for helping me to get my boat out of the water. A lot of fishers weren't that fortunate. Their boats are damaged or missing."

Elin passed an envelope to Jason. He opened it and beamed. It was a gift card to an online engineering supplier website. He had been on the site several times thinking of what equipment he would need to start his practice. He got up to give her a hug as grandpa brought in a couple more chairs for the grandparents. They talked about the tsunami as well as the continued shaking. Everyone had a laugh as it shook a little once more. Jason wondered if Daniel had talked to Elin about his proposal to him. Whether he did or not, it didn't appear to be the subject of their visit.

"So, Emma, you head to the hospital day after tomorrow. Is Jason taking you?"

"I believe so. That is if they don't cancel it because of all this shaking."

"Rosa and I will be taking her there. As far as we've heard, there is no change to the plan."

Emma's phone rang. They all stopped talking. She got up from the table and went into the living room. When she came back to the kitchen she sat down.

"It was Justin. Just checking up on all of us. He said to give you a hug, Elin, so here it comes."

Iris poured Elin a cup of tea as Andrew sat quietly at the table until Jason started talking about the riverside property. The damage was significant. Andrew looked around at everyone as he relaxed a little.

"I found the coolest sketch book at the cottage. Not sure who it belongs to, but the drawings are impressive. The only identifying signature was the initials AW," Emma remarked.

Elin looked over at Andrew, but he didn't say anything, so she was just going to leave that to him. She was not 100% sure that it was his book but from the look on his face, plus, knowing that he had slept there a couple of nights, she thought it was his. He got up and went to the washroom while the rest of them continued to chat about the tsunami.

"I'm going to let Roy and Heather know about the damage. They were looking at the property."

"Rosa and I were considering buying the property as well. It's a fairly large parcel of land, we could even divide it."

"Can I pass that along to Heather?"

"Sure. It's not a secret."

"Ohhhh…does that mean that you are going to buy the property together, Jay?" Emma teased.

"That was what we were thinking. And before you say anything, yes, we are thinking of a life together."

Emma reached over to touch Rosa's hand as she looked down at the table.

"Not quite how we were going to let you all know. But it is done now," Rosa said.

Emma's phone rang again. She got up to take the call, away from the conversations going on at the table.

"Hello," Emma said as she picked up her phone.

"Hi, is this Emma Ryan?"

"Yes, who is calling?"

"It's Mary, I'm confirming your surgery time for day after tomorrow. It will be at 2 pm. We ask that you check into the hospital at 8 am tomorrow."

"Good, I wasn't sure it would be done with the damage done by the tsunami."

"Our ER is pretty busy, but the surgeries are all continuing as scheduled. So, we'll see you soon."

"Yes. It will be one of my last surgeries. They are planning to do both surgeries while I'm there."

"It appears that way. The second one will be early the following week."

"OK. See you tomorrow."

"Bye."

Emma took a minute to look out the window at the beautiful day that followed the tsunami. The deep blue sky with the sun shining on the mountains always made her feel better. She really couldn't explain it, but it gave her a warmth deep inside. She headed back into the kitchen to let them know that everything was a 'go' for her surgery.

Another car pulled up to the Ryan house and Justin hopped out. Daniel had told him to go back to check on everyone and it did not take a lot of convincing. As he came up the stairs, he thought about what the day after tomorrow would bring. He was glad he could be with Emma when she checked into the hospital. She opened the door as he got to the top step, they both just smiled.

"Come in. Join the meeting of the Day After Club, the day after the wave that kept us all awake."

"Well, thank you. Can I get a membership to that club?"

"You had your initiation last night. Welcome to our first meeting."

He gave Emma a hug as they walked into the kitchen. Elin and Andrew looked over at the two of them, exchanging a glance. Elin asked Justin if he needed a place to stay tonight as his old room was waiting for him. He gave her the thumbs up as he looked around the table. The old tension was gone, even after his mother threw Jason out of their old house last night.

Iris and Austin were standing up, so Iris got Justin a cup of tea. After that, the grandparents went to the living room to let the young people talk things out. They would miss the young people if they moved back to their old place.

However, with Jason, Rosa, and Emma living in the house it was bound to get noisier as well as busier. They wondered if they would want them to continue to stay there. Jason came into the living room to tell them to come back to the table. He brought a couple of chairs so they could sit down.

Once everyone gathered at the house was seated in their chairs, Jason gave an envelope to his grandfather. Austin wondered if they were completing their presence there with a gift of some sort. He looked at the envelope, then handed it to his wife. She opened the envelope. A gift card fell out of it. She read the letter then passed it to her husband. Everyone went silent as he read it until Emma felt like she was going to burst.

"Well, what's the answer?"

The grandparents sat there in silence, so Jason took the letter and read it out loud.

"To Iris and Austin Ryan, this letter is to let you know that you have become co-owners, with Jason Jr. and Emma, of the 3519 Elk Drive property once owned by Jason and Alison Ryan. After all the years you took care of Emma and Jason Jr, they have decided to share the property with you. In the event of the property being no longer useful to you, it will revert back to Emma and Jason Jr. Ryan."

"Speech! Speech!" Emma shouted.

The grandparents looked at each other, then Austin stood up.

"Jason, Emma, thank you for your gift. I see the gift card is for a Cruise Line. Iris and I will use that. As for this house, it belongs to both of you."

"No, it belongs to all four of us," Jason added. "We would like you to stay here with us. I know that's a little selfish, but you make things work so well. We want to let you know how much we appreciate all you've done."

"Iris and I are still trying to decide what to do. We still have our property about an hour from here. We have visited it a couple of times. We are here for the summer anyway as we want to be here as Emma recovers. After that, we will make our decision but thank you for all of this."

Emma and Jason got up to hug both of them. It was good enough for today; tomorrow would bring its own story.

www.ingramcontent.com/pod-product-compliance
Lightning Source LLC
La Vergne TN
LVHW010403220526
839361LV00007B/36